They didn't really like each other...

Their only bond was his father. Boris had treated her violently and brutally and yet...to sit with him in a public place, to be the center of attention, was something Polly found stimulating. He was the most dynamic man she'd ever met. Dynamic, vital—virile.

He regarded her across the table levelly, very coolly. "Stop staring," she said at last, aware that her cheeks were going pink.

"I was just trying to see what makes you tick. There's a strong personality in there somewhere."

"Well, you should know one when you see one," she retorted. Their eyes met and suddenly it was as if everything else faded away. Just the two of them in a clash of wills....

The Dark Warrior

by

MARY WIBBERLEY

Harlequin Books

TORONTO • LONDON • NEW YORK • AMSTERDAM
SYDNEY • HAMBURG • PARIS

Original hardcover edition published in 1979
by Mills & Boon Limited

ISBN 0-373-02277-8

Harlequin edition published August 1979

CHAPTER ONE

'HE'S one of the wealthiest men in Europe,' said Ed Welsh. 'And he's virtually a recluse.'

'That *is* a big help,' said Polly, 'so how do I get near enough to the great man to interview him? And why *me* for heaven's sakes, I've only been here a month. I'm not——'

'There's one big difference between you and us,' answered Ed, brushing the ash from his jazzy waistcoat.

'I know—I'm a girl,' retorted Polly.

'Not that, you idiot!' Ed grinned. 'Take a look at this photo.' He handed her a large glossy photograph. She assumed it would be of the man himself, Boris Leander, but it was of a young woman. She nearly dropped it when she saw the face that looked back at her.

'But—but—she's like *me*!' she squeaked. It was uncanny. The fair hair was longer; Polly wore hers in a short curly style that suited her, but the face she looked at might have been her own. Soft and round, large clear eyes, widely set; pert nose, laughing mouth, slender neck—'Good grief!' she said.

'Precisely. And *that's* how we get to him.' Ed was well satisfied with her reaction.

Polly kept looking as she asked: 'Who is she?'

'Who *was* she, dear,' he corrected. 'Leander's wife. She died five years ago in a plane crash—only they never found the body. They'd been married one year. Since then he's never looked at another woman. He was a real playboy up till then, jetting all over the world, yacht in the South of France, racing his own car—you name it, he'd done it. And then—nothing. And we want to know all about what he's been up to since then, because the word is, something big is brewing, something that concerns this town, only everyone's as tight as a clam. He might talk to you. He certainly won't talk to any other reporters. He gave one a good hiding in Italy last year—one of the *paparazzi*, the wide boys who sneak up on you—and the fellow probably deserved it, and he literally threw another one out of a meeting——'

'Say no more,' Polly said faintly. 'I don't think I could cope with a physical attack. I mean, I may be tall and well built, but I'm no judo expert——'

'They were *men*, you idiot,' Ed laughed. 'I don't think he'd attack a woman——'

'I wouldn't like to find out,' she murmured. 'Thanks, but no, thanks.'

'It's arranged,' he said calmly. 'And don't argue. I got you this job.' He looked at her, and grinned, because he knew he'd won.

Polly was silent. Ed had been the saving of her, a good and valued friend of her late father's. And when her father had died six years previously, two years after her mother, he had come to her house, with his wife and daughter, told her she was going to stay with them until she got herself sorted out, talked to her while Zoe, his wife, and Hilary, his daughter, had packed all her things up, and taken her off.

She had been there ever since. Ed was tough and ruthless in his job as editor of the *Wallington Courier*, but he was a softie at heart, and Polly had never ceased to be grateful. She was looking for a flat, helped by Hilary, and a month previously, when a vacancy had come for a junior reporter on the *Courier*, she had got the job—helped a little by Ed's blatant string-pulling.

And now he was throwing at her the job many reporters would give their eye teeth to have. Only she didn't know the first thing about interviewing. She had done a piece on the local over-sixties club, and covered a flower show—and that was it. 'I—I wouldn't know where to start,' she confessed.

Ed pressed the button on his intercom and grinned. 'You're about to get a crash course,' he said. Then, as his secretary answered: 'Jill, send in Pete Macken.'

Polly groaned. 'Please—not *him*,' she wailed. 'He's like a——'

'Ssh! He's the best one to show you the ropes. You've got a week.'

'A *week*! I'll never——'

'Yes, you will.'

'Where do we—I—meet the big man?' she asked quietly.

'Next Tuesday. At the Wallington Arms.'

'I thought you said he was a recluse?'

'He is. But he does emerge occasionally. This is a mayor's reception—don't ask me *why*, but it's all tied up with this hush-hush stuff we're trying to find out about. I'm invited in my capacity as head of the local Samaritans. It's strictly a no-reporters affair—but you're going as my niece.'

Her heart sank. 'But that's dishonest,' she whispered.

'I know, love,' he answered cheerfully. 'Isn't it just? And the big man will put in a brief appearance —and you use all your charm to *get him* talking, right? Understood?'

'But——'

'No buts. I've spoken. Now, here's Pete—come in, lad.'

Polly's apprehension only increased as the week passed. Ed had sworn her to secrecy about the proposed interview with the big man—the way he was referred to in every paper in the land on the rare occasions that he was mentioned—and she couldn't talk about it at home. She sensed it was because Zoe would not approve, and Ed knew it. On the Monday evening she sat in the lounge of their comfortable home, drying her hair with Hilary's dryer, and Zoe looked at her, concerned.

'Are you all right, love?' she asked.

'Fine,' Polly lied. 'Just a headache, that's all.' I'll be better this time tomorrow, she thought, when it's all over. She smiled at Mrs Welsh to reassure her.

'I know how to cure that,' said Hilary. 'Come with me to the disco tonight. You know Alan's friend's dying to meet you——'

'I know, I'd love to, normally, but I think I'll get an early night tonight. I want to be fresh for this meeting tomorrow.' That was all they knew—that Polly was going to a meeting at the Wallington Arms with Ed. That was all she had been allowed to tell them. She felt bad about it; they were, all three, good and loyal, and had helped her through a bad time when the first sense of loss had been total and overwhelming. Now she was nearly back to normal, and it was thanks to them, and she felt shabby about the deceit. She combed her nearly dry hair, and Hilary sighed.

'It's not fair,' she wailed. 'Look at that—comb, flick, and bob's your uncle, and me, if I don't put curlers in every night, I look a fright!'

Polly looked severely at Hilary. 'I'll swop you any day,' she said. 'You can sweep yours up, and back into some super styles if you want. I shall never look like that——'

'Quiet, both of you!' Zoe Welsh had heard enough. 'You want your heads banging together. You've *both* got nice hair.'

Hilary pulled a face and winked at Polly. 'Yes, Mummy, sorry, Mummy——' she ducked a well aimed cushion and said to Polly:

'Come and help me choose something to wear, love. As a matter of fact, I was wondering, if you're not going out tonight—er—the snazzy cheesecloth blouse——'

'You can borrow it,' said Polly. 'Come on.' They went out laughing.

Later she lay in bed, and wondered if you could get butterflies in the stomach twelve hours before an ordeal, and if so, would they get worse as the time approached? She punched her pillow, sat up, switched on the light and picked up a horror thriller that Hilary had lent her. It might at least give her a different kind of nightmare . . .

The morning came at last, and she went down to breakfast with the feeling of imminent execution. Could she plead migraine—broken leg—insanity?

Ed greeted her cheerily and winked before returning to his bacon, sausage and eggs. Polly winced and looked away. Toast was all she could manage, and perhaps a cup of tea. . . .

'Look smart now,' he warned. Zoe was busy in the kitchen. 'What about that yellow thing—you know, the trouser suit? That'll do nicely.'

'Yes, Ed,' she said dispiritedly.

'Cheer up,' he urged. 'I wouldn't get you into anything nasty, you know that. It's just a little job, that's all.'

'I know. But what if I let you down?'

'No harm done! It'll be a miracle if he even talks to you. Better men than you——'

'Thanks,' she said dryly.

'You know what I mean! Better *reporters* than you,

then, have tried and failed. It's just a little gamble.'

That made her feel a trace better, but not much. Enough to eat, and enjoy, two pieces of crisp toast and marmalade. And three hours later, she met Ed outside the Wallington Arms, determined not to let him down. He had done so much for her, the least she could do was try.

'Ready?' he said.

'Aye, aye, sir.' She took his arm, took a deep breath —and they went in.

Polly kept to fruit juice. She needed a clear head. She was stuck in a corner by elderly ex-councillor Potter and his middle-aged charity-organising wife, listening to a boring account of a fight to prevent a new estate of houses being built on parkland outside Wallington, and trying to keep an interested expression on her face— and wishing that Ed hadn't abandoned her to their tender mercies—when there was a commotion at the door, a flurry of activity, a to-ing and fro-ing, and she froze. The reception had been on for an hour, it was time for the big man to arrive. Could it be him? She forgot to listen and look interested, and fixed her eyes on the door.

The mayor, a small pompous builder, came in first, wearing his chain of office, and clearing his throat importantly. 'Ladies and gentlemen,' he announced, 'Mr Leander is on his way in. Please—no fuss.' He looked as though he was going to make a fuss. He looked as though he might burst with pride.

Polly's neighbours began talking quickly, the woman patting her hair, saying: 'Do I look all right, George?' and her husband straightening his tie, turning to Polly.

'This is a big moment for Wallington,' he said,

'Indeed yes,' she murmured. She had no tie to straighten, and she wasn't going to pat her hair. She just wanted to go home.

Then he walked in. She had seen only a photograph of him that had been taken ten years previously, in his heyday as a racing driver, and that had been slightly blurred, but it was unmistakably him. It was as though everyone faded away, and she saw only him. He was tall, taller than anyone else there, and he was dark, and tanned and devastatingly attractive. All man, immaculately dressed in grey suit, white shirt, dark tie. He stood there, looking round him, not smiling, and the mayor rushed forward, practically tripping over his feet to greet him, to shake hands—and Boris Leander looked across at Polly, and for a full five seconds his eyes were upon her. She felt as if she had just received a huge electric shock. Those eyes—— She took a deep breath, and croaked, in answer to Mrs Potter, who had hissed: 'Isn't he handsome, my dear?'

'Yes, he is.' Handsome wasn't exactly the right word, but Polly was too transfixed to argue. Handsome implied smooth good looks, a big smile. His face was rugged and tough, the face of an adventurer—or a pirate; green eyes, sea green, shadowed, a strong straight nose, wide mouth, hard chin. And he hadn't yet smiled.

And *she* had to try and talk to him. She knew she wouldn't dare. She screamed silently, inwardly, for Ed to return. Where was he? He had sloped out minutes before, after being in a huddle by the door with three other men, and now there was no sign of him. Perhaps he had gone to the gents.

'Excuse me.' She put her drink down on a table, smiled at Mr and Mrs Potter, and skirted round the group that had formed round Boris Leander, and out of the door. She ran along the corridor towards the toilets, and Ed stepped out from behind a pillar, grabbed her arm, exclaiming: 'Thank God you've come out!'

'What's the matter?' she whispered. '*He*'s arrived!'

'I know. I'm keeping out of the way. Some fool recognised me—if it gets to him that I'm on a paper I'd be out on my ear, and he'd be doing the throwing. You're on your own, ducky. Don't let me down, for God's sake. I'll be in the bar downstairs.' He patted her hand and began to move away.

'You can't——' she squealed—'help!' She swallowed hard. 'You can't *leave* me—I——'

'You're safe. *You're* a woman. I'm getting out while I've still got my arms and legs and nose intact. Don't forget—the bar. And good luck, love.'

He was gone. Polly felt like someone who had been neatly stranded on a desert island and was watching the boat vanishing over the horizon.

She went into the ladies' room, put on more lipstick, a squirt of Hilary's best perfume, borrowed in return for the blouse, and went back into the reception. The longer she waited, the more difficult it would be. The fact that Ed thought she looked like Boris Leander's late wife was hardly any consolation. Ed hadn't seen the look the big man had given her. It had been almost frightening.

He was talking, surrounded by a fluttering throng of local dignitaries, and they were listening. When a man like that spoke, Polly thought, everyone listened attentively. '—and so I'm passing through, and thought it would be rather nice to meet the people in the town my grandmother lived in as a child.' He finished the sentence—and smiled. Two things registered with Polly. One—he was lying. His grandmother might well have lived in Wallington, but that wasn't the real reason he was there. And the second thing that registered was his smile. It changed his face, it made him look human. Polly mentally apologised to the effusive Mrs Potter, who was hovering on the fringe of the group. He was handsome, when he smiled. What a waste, she thought —to be a recluse, a man like that. She sighed a little sigh, and Boris Leander turned to face her, as though he had been waiting for her, and said:

'Good afternoon. Are you a local resident?'

'Yes.' She was surprised, now that the moment was upon her, to find she could actually speak. Perhaps the adrenalin's working overtime, she thought. All eyes were upon her. She smiled at him. He was dishy, no two ways about it. 'I live in Chatford Avenue—about a mile away. Where was your grandmother born?'

'In the old part of town. I'm afraid the house has

gone now. I went to see this morning.' He shrugged. 'That's progress.' Someone cut in, asking him where he was staying, and the attention was diverted from Polly. But he had noticed her, and he wasn't hostile. There was a chance, slender admittedly, to talk to him again, but only if she could get him away from the crowd. Had he noticed the resemblance? And would it help or hinder her? Nothing had shown in his face save a polite interest; the great man unbending to speak to a young woman, no more. Polly went and found her glass and stood by the window, mercifully alone. She needed to think. How did she open? 'Oh, Mr Leander, it's so interesting you being here, and I'm sure your granny did live here, but what are you planning? A big take-over of the town? A new factory?' She grimaced. He could probably eject girl reporters with one gaze from those cold green eyes. They *were* cold. They had even been cold when he smiled. The smile had transformed his face, but left the eyes untouched. She shivered, and wondered when she could escape, if only for a bite at the bar. It was gone twelve. He would leave soon, he must. He wasn't the type to spend much time on the little people of Wallington, even if he did have a motive in coming here, winning them over. . . .

Right, she thought, that's it. Now or never. I shall plunge in and say: 'May I have a word with you, Mr Leander?' And if he said no, she had tried.

She took a firm, deep breath, put down her glass, and his voice said: 'May I have a word with you?'

She stopped, she looked, up and up, to his face, and she thought she was having an hallucination.

'What?' she said, in a teeny voice.

'I said may I have a word with you?' The throng remained at a respectful distance. She would be the talk of Wallington tomorrow.

'Yes, of course. Here?'

'No, somewhere a little—quieter.' He grinned faintly. This time it reached his eyes, and for a moment they were no longer cold. 'Would you have lunch with me?'

She wanted to pinch herself, because that was what you were supposed to do when you thought you were dreaming. It wasn't happening. It couldn't be....

'I'd—love to,' she said faintly.

'I have a suite here. I prefer to eat there—if you don't mind.'

'Oh.' It was a small oh. Ed had said he had never looked at another woman, but the small warning bells rang at the back of her mind. Supposing he made a pass at her? Suppose he——

'If you prefer, we can go out. There's a good restaurant about five miles away, I believe?'

'Yes, there is. Thank you. Er—how——' She raised an eyebrow towards the clusters of people who were talking as though fascinated by each other's conversation, but just waiting for the moment when Mr Leander might care to join them again.

'Watch me. Just stay where you are, I'll be back.' He turned and left her standing there and joined the little group that contained the mayor. Within three minutes the room was empty, save for the two of them.

'Just like that?' she said.

'Yes.' His mouth quirked into a half smile. 'I said I had a lunch appointment, was delighted to have met them, and asked the mayor and his wife over for drinks this evening.'

Polly was suddenly nervous. It was all happening too fast, and too easily. She ran her tongue over her dry lips. How did she let Ed know? No one had seen them together, except briefly, and it might just have been that they had walked in at the same time, so no one would think to tell him that his young lady had gone off with Mr Leander. Then she remembered. They would have to go through the bar going out. A reassuring wink was all that was needed. She smiled to herself at the thought, and Boris Leander said: 'Are you ready to leave?'

'Yes.'

He picked up her bag from the table and handed it to her. 'My car's outside. Let's go.'

She sailed through the bar, and Ed nearly fell off his chair. Polly smiled at him, then they were going through the door and out into the pale sunshine of a July day.

He led her over to a grey Daimler parked at the side of the hotel, opened her door for her, got in himself, and said: 'Tell me about yourself, please. I don't even know your name.'

'Polly Summers.'

'Do you work?'

'Yes. I'm a—secretary.' She had been, up until a month ago. She still did a lot of typing in the office, so it wasn't strictly a lie.

'Fine. Happy in your work?'

'Yes. Are you?'

He laughed at that. They were driving through the main street, and she closed her eyes as they passed the office of the *Wallington Courier*. 'As much as anyone can be,' he answered.

'But you—forgive me—you are rarely seen. Everyone was very surprised when you decided to come to Wallington.'

'Were they? I'm a man of impulse, Miss Summers. I was in this part of the world, thought I'd like to see the town, and I came. It seemed a nice idea to meet the people on my visit, that was all.'

'There's more,' she said. He could hardly throw her out of the car now. Well, he could. He could just stop it and tell her to get out, and she would simply walk back to the office and tell them what had happened. No one would be surprised. Their only surprise would be in knowing she had got that far with him.

'Really? What makes you say that?'

'An instinct. Putting two and two together, if you like. Something in the air.'

'You're very shrewd—I like that. I'm surrounded by people who tend to agree with everything I say, and never question it. It can get very tedious at times.'

'Don't you think it's only natural? People are probably frightened of the power you wield.'

'And are you?'

Polly only had to consider it for a second. 'No,' she answered, 'I'm not.'

She looked sideways at him. 'The worst thing you can do to me is stop the car and tell me to get out. I'd live.'

'I have no intention of doing so,' he answered smoothly. 'That would be appalling bad manners. You have accepted my lunch invitation, and that is that.'

'Why did you ask me?'

He slowed the car as they neared the Fourways Restaurant.

'Because I have a proposition to make to you. It will take time to explain fully—but I hope very much that you will accept.'

CHAPTER TWO

HE waited until they were seated and had ordered before he spoke again of the proposition.

'What I am about to tell you is in the strictest confidence,' he said. 'May I have your word that what I am going to tell you will go no further?'

'Yes. But I must make one thing clear. I don't know what this "proposition" is, Mr Leander, and I may say no.'

'Of course you may. In that case I shall return you to the town after lunch, say goodbye, and that will be that. I promise you now it is nothing illegal or immoral. Do you believe me?'

She nodded. 'Yes.'

The waiter arrived with the hors-d'œuvres, and when he had gone, Boris Leander spoke again. 'My father lives in a remote part of the Border country. He is nearly seventy-seven, and several weeks ago suffered a massive brain haemorrhage——' he paused at her instinctive indrawn breath of empathy. That was how her father had died. . . .

'I am not seeking sympathy, Miss Summers, I have adjusted to the situation now, and the fact that the doctors have told me he has possibly only weeks to live. He is paralysed, and cannot talk.' His face as he spoke was expressionless. He might have been talking about a stranger.

'And this is where my proposition comes in. I was married six years ago. My wife was killed a year after our wedding—her death broke my father completely, shattered him. In fact for a long time he refused to accept that she had died. Her body was never found.' Polly found herself clenching her hands under the table. She already knew this, that was the terrible thing. And she was having to pretend she was hearing it for the first time. It made her feel a hypocrite.

'And now—I saw you this morning, and I knew that there was a way to make my father's last weeks happy——'

She knew now what was coming. She wanted to scream, to run, to escape, but she was compelled to sit where she was, eyes wide—and helpless. 'My wife is—was—your double. There is no other way to explain the uncanny resemblance. Save for a different hairstyle, you might be her.' He paused, as if waiting for what she might say.

'You want me to pretend to be your wife?' she whispered.

'Yes.'

'But how?'

'Travel with me to his home tomorrow. I will tell him all that is necessary. All you will be expected to do is sit beside his bed to talk to him gently, that is all. And in return I shall recompense you fully. I shall give you ten thousand pounds, to be paid into your bank immediately.'

The amount left her literally speechless. She had never even seen that much, let alone thought of having it. Then she found her voice. 'No,' she said.

'No?' For the first time a trace of emotion showed in his face.

'Not that I refuse—but the money! I can't allow you to give it——'

'Miss Summers, it is nothing to me. I would pay ten times that amount if I thought my father's last weeks would be happy——'

'I'll do it for nothing—my father died six months ago of the same thing. All I ask is something like—oh, two hundred pounds to buy some decent clothes, and cover expenses.'

There was a silence that stretched and grew. 'Miss Summers,' Boris Leander said at last, 'you are a remarkable young woman.'

'No, I'm not.' Polly shook her head. 'I'm very ordinary. But an amount like that would change my life too much. I've never had much, but then I've never wanted it. I don't think money buys happiness.'

A small smile touched his mouth. 'And very wise.'

She didn't know what was happening to her. She had intended to refuse—she had, after all, come into his life under false pretences—but suddenly it had seemed right. For all his money, Boris Leander was an unhappy man. It showed not in what he said, not on his face, but in something that lay behind his eyes. A secret pain. She wanted to tell him then that she was a reporter who had been deliberately sent, using her remarkable resemblance to his late wife, to try and find out all about him. The opportunity to do so was now being handed to her on a plate—and he would never know. She looked at him, and the moment passed. It was a significant moment in her life. She should have told him. . . .

'I'll come with you tomorrow.' She pushed away her empty plate as the waiter returned. 'I'd appreciate it if you'd drop me off at home after this meal. I have arrangements to make.'

'Of course.' He raised his wine glass. 'I am very grateful to you, Miss Summers.'

'Hadn't you better call me Polly?'

'Thank you—Polly. My late wife's name was Crystal. Only my father will call you by it, of course. My staff at the house will know exactly who you are.'

'Crystal,' she repeated slowly.

He looked away briefly, as if even the name had the power to hurt him. Hurriedly she went on: 'You say your house is on the borders—presumably of Scotland and England?'

'Yes.' A faint smile, as if he appreciated her tact. 'Very secluded. No one knows of it—which suits me well. I enjoy my privacy.'

Do you? she thought. I wonder. Instead she said: 'As long as you have plenty of books—have you? I enjoy browsing.'

'Ah, you do? Then we have something in common. Tell me, who are your favourite writers?'

They launched into a discussion of various books and their authors, found they had several favourites in common—and disagreed about others. And the lunch passed all too quickly.

This was the tricky time. Suppose someone had already mentioned Ed's name as being the editor of the local weekly? And said where he lived?

Polly hated the necessary deception, but asked Boris Leander to drop her by the supermarket in Wallington —and gave him her telephone number. Ed would know what to do. The only snag was, what on earth did she tell him?

She had given her word to Boris Leander, and had no intention of breaking it. On the other hand both Ed and his wife had the right to know where she was going. As they neared the town, she said: 'I'm staying with friends of my late parents until I get a flat of my own. They have a right to know why I'm going off into the blue with a man I've only just met.'

'Indeed they have. Tell them the truth—or part of it. Say I have asked you to work for me for a couple of months. We both discovered a great interest in books. Could you then bend the truth a little and say it is because I need my library of antique books cataloguing? That is also true—I do. And you may do some, if you so wish.'

'I used to work in a library,' she said thoughtfully, 'after I left school—they know that. Very well,' she smiled. 'You can drop me here.'

He slowed the car. 'If you need me for anything, I am at the Wallington Arms. I shall make sure any of your calls are put through immediately.'

'Thank you. What time shall I be ready in the morning?'

'Eleven? What about your job? Can you get leave? Would you like me to telephone your boss——'

'No,' she said hastily, 'I can fix that. Goodbye for now.'

He opened her door by leaning across her. For a brief moment his face was only inches away, and she could smell the cool tang of his aftershave, could have touched him. . . .

'*Au revoir*,' he said. 'I will call you, tonight.'

She watched him drive away, and went, rather shakily, into the supermarket. It was all assuming the proportions of a dream.

'My *dear*!' exclaimed Zoe Welsh, Ed's having kittens —you'd better phone him at the paper—and when you've done that, you'd better tell *me* what you've been up to.'

Polly went and dialled the office and was put through immediately to Ed. 'What on *earth*——' he began. 'I've been going quietly——'

'Just listen. He approached me, took me out to lunch, and we talked. He's offered me a job.'

The line nearly exploded. '*What!*'

'He's ringing me tonight. I'd rather not talk over the phone. What time will you be home?'

'I'm coming now,' he said, and hung up.

'He's on his way,' Polly told Zoe.

'He's *what*? He never leaves there before six.'

'He is doing. We'd better get the kettle on. I've a feeling he's going to need a good strong cup of tea, with plenty of sugar—for shock.' Polly gave Zoe a rueful little smile. 'Then I can explain to you both at once.'

Zoe sat down. 'Oh, my God,' she said.

Polly went to put the kettle on, the words of the old nursery rhyme coming back to her, making her giggle. 'Polly put the kettle on, Polly put the kettle on....' It was more as a relief from tension than anything else. Ed had sounded not exactly angry, but .... They waited.

He walked in five minutes later, stared hard at Polly, and said: 'Right, lass, out with it.'

'It's quite simple. He's offered me a dream of a job for a few weeks, cataloguing his collection of antique books at his house in the Border country.'

Ed sat down heavily on a kitchen chair. Polly poured him a beaker of strong tea, took one look at him, added three heaped teaspoons of sugar, and sat down opposite him. 'My God,' he said softly. 'Just like that. And I never dreamed you'd get even anywhere near him——'

'You didn't. But you took me——'

'It was a slim chance, that was all. Phew!' he whistled softly. 'It's *incredible*!'

'But,' interrupted Zoe, 'why *you*, love? I mean— don't get me wrong, but people like him don't pick up girls at receptions and offer them jobs. I don't like it, Ed.' She glared at her husband.

He pulled a face. 'I'm not sure if I do, either. I'd better tell you exactly what we were up to.' And he explained to his wife about Polly's startling resemblance to Boris Leander's late wife, and the hope they had had of getting an interview on the strength of it. When he had finished, Zoe shook her head even more firmly.

'No,' she said. 'I like it even less now. I mean, the man could be——' she pursed her lips—'you *know* what I mean.'

'I do.'

Polly spoke. She had listened for long enough. 'Look, it's not like that, I promise,' she said. 'Really. He's not a wolf. We had lunch, and he's a perfect gentle-man. There's lots of staff at the house, and—er—relatives——' well, one, she added mentally, but I can't say who, and it's not really a lie because I've been sworn to secrecy, 'and it's a chance of a life-time——'

'I can't have you taking the risk,' said Ed. 'Sorry, love, it *is* the chance of a lifetime, as you say, to find out everything about him—and normally I'd be like a cat with two tails at the thought of getting all the in-side info about a man like that. My God, the Fleet Street papers would give thousands for that kind of story—but it's *you*, and we're like parents to you at the moment——'

'But I'm going,' said Polly.

Her words fell into the sudden, startled silence. Zoe and Ed looked at one another, then at Polly.

'You can't!' Ed wailed. 'It kills me to say it, but——'

'Then don't.' She smiled at them both very gently. 'It's all right, I know what I'm doing. And if you want, you can meet him tomorrow, before I go.'

Ed's mouth opened, and closed. He was never lost for words. He was now.

It was Zoe who spoke for him. 'If she's determined,' she said, 'then I shall definitely insist——'

'But I can't,' he answered. 'He may recognise me——'

'But he won't know *me*,' cut in Zoe. She could be as

determined as Ed, when she chose. 'I'll go. And if I don't like him I shall tell him so.'

She would too. Polly bit her lip to hide a smile. She could see Zoe wiping the floor—or trying to—with Boris Leander, if she didn't like the look of him. The scene could well be awesome. She didn't imagine anyone had ever dared speak to Boris Leander with less than reverence in their voice before. But Zoe had once tackled a local bully-boy councillor at a village meeting over some proposed building of a car park on a playground, and virtually demolished him in public. The man had not been the same since.

Ed cleared his throat. 'Well——' he began, doubtfully, 'I don't——'

'Nonsense,' said Zoe crisply. 'You got Polly into this. Don't argue with me now. Go and phone this man, Polly. Tell him I want to meet him, tonight if possible. Let's see what he says.'

'Polly nodded. 'Very well. At his hotel?'

'Anywhere he likes.'

She heard them arguing as she left the kitchen, closing the door firmly after her. Then she found the number of the Wallington Arms, and began to dial.

Boris Leander sent his car for them at eight, and ten minutes later Polly and Zoe were sitting in the small but comfortable living room of his suite at the hotel. Zoe looked at Polly, and mouthed: 'Where is he?' and Polly shrugged, mouthing back: 'Search me.' They had been taken up by a chambermaid, who had assured them Mr Leander would not be a moment, and would they wait.

Then the door opened, and he walked in. He walked in, and he filled that small room with his presence, and Polly saw the instant shock of reaction in Zoe's eyes, and waited.

'Forgive me,' he said. 'An urgent telephone call. Mrs Welsh? How do you do?' He strode over to her and shook hands. 'Good evening, Polly. May I give you both a drink?' He went over to where various bottles were ranged on a table with glasses.

'A Martini for me—very dry,' said Zoe, recovering. Polly could see why. He wore a stunningly plain black sweater and grey slacks. He was broader shouldered without a concealing jacket, the sweater emphasised his tan, and his green eyes, normally so cold, were warm as he looked at them both. My God, Polly thought, he can lay on the charm when he chooses. And it seemed he chose.

'I'll have a rum and pep,' she said.

'Fine.' He poured, and Zoe rolled her eyes at Polly behind his broad back. The look said it all. It said: he's gorgeous—but I don't trust him an inch.

He handed them their glasses, poured a brandy for himself, and raised his glass. 'Your good health,' he said. 'Mrs Welsh, I know why you have come tonight, and I wish to thank you for doing so. Polly will have explained what I want her to do, and you have naturally come to see why I should ask a perfect stranger to catalogue my books for me—and I don't blame you in the slightest for wanting to check up on me.' He smiled gently, and sat down opposite Zoe. 'I would do just the same, were it to happen to my daughter. In fact, I appreciate your concern.'

'Then you can also appreciate, Mr Leander,' said Zoe, 'the fact that I find it a little odd—to say the least —that you should meet Polly at a reception, a girl on her own, take her out to lunch and ask her what you have, when it's obvious to me anyway that a man in your position, and with your wealth—forgive me for speaking so frankly, but Polly is as dear to me as my own daughter—can have anyone he wants to do his bidding at any time. Frankly, I don't see why you chose her.'

There was a brief, pregnant silence. Polly braced herself inwardly for the explosion. Boris Leander was not the man you spoke to like that—ever.

There was none. Whatever else he was—and he was undoubtedly a man of great personal power—he also possessed superb control of his emotions. He nodded. 'Mrs Welsh,' he said, 'you give me no choice but to tell you the truth. The absolute truth, and if, when I have finished telling you, you still have your doubts, I will then ask you something.' He stood up and took Zoe's empty glass. 'May I give you another drink?'

'No, thanks. I want a clear head.'

The faintest trace of a smile touched his mouth. 'I see. I would appreciate if you understand that what I am about to tell you is in strict confidence.'

'Very well.' Zoe sat back composedly. 'I'm listening.'

Polly glanced from her to him. She might as well not have been there, for all the notice either took of her. He began to speak, quietly at first, and she listened, and Zoe listened—intently—and when he had finished he produced a photograph from a drawer and handed it to Zoe.

There were tears in her eyes when she looked up from it to him. 'I understand now,' she said.

'Thank you. I will now ask you the question. If you are still unhappy about my proposition, would you also like to come to the house with Polly?'

She shook her head. 'I have a husband and daughter to look after, Mr Leander,' she said. 'And in any case, it won't be necessary. I believe you——' She hesitated. 'I know now why Polly said she would go.' She looked at Polly. 'Of course you must, love,' she said quietly.

'Thank you. Another drink?'

'I think I need it.' She smiled at him.

'Polly?'

'No, thanks.'

'I would like to leave in the morning,' he went on. 'We will reach Leander House after lunch.' He began to write on a pad, and handed the sheet to Zoe. 'There is the full address and telephone number. I would like to call them now and prepare my staff for our arrival. Will you excuse me for a minute?'

'Of course.' When he had gone, Zoe looked across at Polly. 'What on earth do we tell Ed?' she asked.

'I don't know,' Polly confessed.

'I'll think of something. As long as I'm happy, that'll

be good enough for him. Are you going to—to——'
she stopped.

Polly knew what she wanted to say, yet could not put
into words. 'No,' she answered softly. 'This is a job
separate from anything else. I know what Ed wanted
—wants—about Boris Leander, he wants to find out
everything about him. But don't you see, I could never
write about anything I see or hear at his house?'

'Oh, I see all right,' Zoe smiled. 'I may be Ed's wife,
but it doesn't make me believe that newspapers have
the right to pry into people's lives.' She nodded. 'We'll
think of something to tell Ed——'

She stopped as the man walked into the room again.
Someone had once asked Polly to define the word
'charisma'. She now knew the simplest way to describe
it! Boris Leander. He had it—a personal quality that
enables an individual to impress others. By his very
walking into the room something changed. Wherever
he went people would be immensely aware of him—
whether into a vast room with dozens of people, or just
a few. It was an electricity in the atmosphere, and he
brought it with him.

He looked at them both and smiled. 'All is arranged,'
he said. 'May I ask you both to stay to dinner with
me?'

Polly looked at Zoe, and Zoe looked at Polly.
'We-ell——' began Zoe, thinking no doubt of the
casserole she had left in the oven, and the waiting Ed.
Then a swift decision. May I phone home?'

'But of course. This way. The telephone is in my

bedroom.' Boris Leander opened the door for her and showed her, closing it firmly before coming back to Polly.

'I thought you'd invited the mayor over this evening?' she said.

'Indeed I had. But at six-thirty. When you phoned I rearranged the evening slightly, had them leave before eight—they were quite happy. Your visit was more important.'

She digested that in silence for a moment. Did he always make people do as he wanted? They were quite happy, he had said. Would they dare be otherwise? And had he worked on Zoe in the same way? She had watched them talking, and now realised something that had subconsciously struck her at the time. He was like an actor, a superb actor, putting on a performance. She looked at him. Even when he had told her about his father, nothing had showed. He could have been talking about a stranger. Perhaps he possessed no emotions—only the ability to manipulate people.

She felt suddenly cold. What kind of man *was* he? 'Tell me,' he said softly, 'why do you look so worried?'

'Do I?' She smiled. 'I was just thinking.'

'About me?'

'Perhaps. Are you a mind-reader as well?'

'I may be.' He smiled slightly. 'In business it helps.'

'I'm sure it does. Is that why you told Zoe everything?'

'I told her because I trust her—and because I knew

it was the only way to make her let you come with an easy mind.'

'Is it so important?' she asked softly.

'Yes.'

Then Zoe returned. She beamed, 'All's well.'

'Then I shall ask for the menu to be sent up. I prefer to dine up here for obvious reasons.' He smiled at Polly. 'This time you have a chaperone.' She felt herself, quite absurdly of course, going pink. She didn't look *that* naïve, she hoped. He pressed a bell by the window and crossed over to sit opposite them. 'The food here is quite decent,' he said, 'and after we have eaten and talked, I shall have my driver take you home.'

'You know, Mr Leander,' said Zoe, 'you're quite a mystery man. I must confess it's very strange to feel I'm actually going to dine with you.'

Polly quaked inwardly at Zoe's statement. She never minced words—and then he laughed, genuinely amused. 'Am I? Do you know something? I don't *feel* any different from anyone else. I'm a very private person, that's all.' He shrugged. 'I prefer my affairs to be my own business, and nobody else's. Is that so mysterious?'

Zoe pulled a wry face. 'Well—no,' she admitted, 'but a man in your position can hardly expect the world not to be interested in him.'

He seemed to digest that for a few moments, and before he could speak they were interrupted by a waiter with menu and pad. Which meant, as far as Polly could see, that he had arranged beforehand for one to be brought up when he rang. Which meant he had been confident they would stay. She looked at him as Zoe studied the ornate menu, and asked the waiter a question about an item. He sat there, quiet, still, waiting; a very powerful, formidable man.

The orders were given, the waiter left, and Boris Leander poured them more drinks. He continued speaking as though there had been no interruption: 'If the world is interested in me, it is because of only one thing—money. I dare to make money. The newspapers consider anyone who does to be fair game for their pens.' He smiled softly. 'I don't like newspapers, or what they say.'

'We'd be in a poor way without them,' retorted Zoe.

'Indeed yes—if they kept strictly to the news. Study any one paper on any day. Except for perhaps the *Financial Times*, if you analyse their content, a good half is devoted to gossip and speculation about people's private lives. Is it necessary? Would you like, say, a personal conversation you had with a friend reported in detail—and probably exaggerated out of all proportion?'

Zoe held up her hands in mock surrender. 'Truce,' she said. 'I can see I'm not going to win any arguments with you.'

His face changed. 'Forgive me. You are both my guests. What an appalling host you must think me.' He stood up to take Zoe's almost empty glass from her. 'You deserve another drink. It is the least I can do.' As he uncapped the bottle he half turned. 'It is just that once—certain newspapers published something totally unforgivable, and it altered my life in a way I will not begin to explain.' He walked over to hand Zoe's glass to her. 'But I promise, hand on heart, I shall not mention the subject again. I shall be the attentive host, and you will not, I think, find fault.'

Zoe smiled at him. It would be difficult not to, thought Polly wryly. The hardness was well concealed. The mask of civilisation that had so briefly slipped was back in place. 'Right,' agreed Zoe. 'You mix a mean Martini, Mr Leander. I'm more than a little woozy already.'

'Then we must look after you. It wouldn't be fitting if you returned home to your husband slightly—er—woozy. What would he think of my character then?'

It was the danger moment. Any second now, Polly sensed he would ask the next, polite, casual question—what does your husband do, Mrs Welsh? And it would be disastrous. Quickly, brightly, she turned to Zoe.

'Zoe, love, I must go and powder my nose before dinner, coming?'

'My private bathroom is the other side of the bedroom.' Boris Leander stood up to open the door for them both as they walked—very steadily—towards it.

When they returned, having rehearsed several conversational openings to keep him away from the subject of Ed, the dinner had arrived, a table was set, and the waiter was putting the finishing touches to the cutlery. Their ploy was not needed. He entertained them throughout dinner with incidents from his life travelling the world. He was cool, controlled, witty, never hogging the conversation—and at one point Polly found herself watching him. There was something lacking, yet she didn't know what it was.

The whole situation was unreal anyway. She had met him that day, was now dining with him, a man of mystery most journalists would give their right arms to interview—and there was nothing sinister about him at all, as had been hinted at in some of the more lurid tabloids.

And yet.... What was it? Suddenly she thought she knew what it was. He had turned slightly, to ask Zoe if she wanted more potatoes, Zoe had answered, smiling, making a laughing remark about getting fat, to which he had replied swiftly with a complimentary reference to her slim figure, and his smile had been pleasant—but Polly had seen his eyes. The smile was not there. It had happened before, at the lunchtime meeting, now it was subtly different. There was nothing showing in his eyes save a hooded blankness. Inside, he had no emotions. And if that were so, and it seemed frighteningly possible, the puzzle remained. Why was he so concerned about keeping his dying father happy? Did anything really matter to him at all?

Polly wondered what she was venturing into. Yet it was too late to back out now. She was committed.

CHAPTER THREE

THE ring came at the doorbell, and Zoe hugged Polly. 'Off you go, love,' she said, 'Phone when you arrive, won't you?'

'I will.'

'And—good luck.'

'Thanks.'

Zoe opened the door, and a fair-haired quiet-looking man dressed in immaculate grey chauffeur's uniform, complete with peaked cap, was waiting. He lifted his cap politely. 'Miss Summers? My name is Denvers. May I take your luggage?'

'Yes.' Polly indicated the two suitcases in the hall. She swallowed hard, took a deep breath, and gave Zoe a last hug. She felt absurdly as if she were going to cry. 'What am I doing?' she whispered, as Denvers walked towards the gate, laden.

'I'm not sure myself, my dear, but it'll work out, you'll see.'

'I wish I had your confidence.' Denvers was standing now by the open gate after having put her cases in the boot of the Daimler. 'Ed's fairly happy with your report?'

'Mmm, enough. He's bursting with curiosity, senses there's more than we're telling, but I can clam up when

38

I want. The main thing is I've reassured him of Leander's honourable intentions. Off you go, dear, don't keep them waiting.' They kissed, and Zoe stood by the door as Polly went down the path towards the car.

Ten minutes later they were in the car park of the Wallington Arms. Denvers turned round to Polly and slid the partition back. 'Mr Leander is ready, miss. Would you prefer to wait here while I go in for him?' He had a pleasant smile that lit his blue eyes.

'Yes, thank you.' She sat back. I'm mad, she thought, quite mad. How on earth can I pretend to be someone else? It seemed fairly sane yesterday, to help someone very ill, but soon it will be reality. She wanted to run, to escape——

'Good morning.' The door had opened, and she looked blindly at Boris Leander, not really seeing him, panic-stricken.

'Oh!' was all she could manage.

He frowned. 'Are you all right?' He was in now, and Denvers had closed the door and was walking round to the driver's seat.

'No,' she said, in a small voice. 'It's—I can't——'

He was sitting beside her, not too near, and he turned towards her. 'You feel nervous about what you intend to do.' It was not a question, it was a statement.

'Nervous? That's putting it too mildly. I'm terrified! Look, Mr Leander, it's—the whole situation is absurd——'

'It is bizarre. It is unusual, yes. But not absurd. It will work, and you will ease my father's last weeks in a

way you cannot imagine.' His voice was soothing,
almost hypnotic, and Polly found to her surprise that
the uncertainty was slipping away rapidly.

She tried one last feeble protest. 'It's—a—
deceit——'

'For the highest reasons.' He did something totally
unexpected. He took hold of Polly's hand, covering
it with his own larger one. It was a very strong hand,
and warm, long-fingered, well shaped. 'I am asking
you. I never beg anyone—I am too proud. But I ask
you—please.'

There was a small full silence. It was almost as if
power flowed from him to her, filling her with a kind of
calm. His words had shaken her. For a moment she
glimpsed humanity in him.

'Yes, I know. It's all right. I suppose it was just a
final little panic.' She smiled shakily at him. 'Can we
go?'

'We're on our way.' He took his hand away and
leaned forward to open the partition. 'Right, Denvers.
Ready when you are.'

'Right you are, sir.' The partition slid closed, Boris
Leander sat back in his seat, looked at Polly.

'Sit back and relax. It's a long journey, but you'll
find it comfortable, I trust. And your every need will
be attended to at Leander House. There is an excellent
housekeeper there, Mrs Harris——' His voice drifted
on, calm, reassuring, telling her about the house and
the staff who worked there, describing the nearby village; and Polly listened, asking the occasional ques-

tion as it seemed necessary, and she was surprised to feel the car slowing, going off the motorway after what seemed only minutes. She looked at her watch. They had been travelling for nearly two hours.

'Lunch,' said Boris Leander, sensing her surprise. 'I prefer not to eat at motorway restaurants if I can avoid it. I have booked a meal at a rather nice hotel near here.'

'I don't feel hungry,' she said, and it was quite true. She thought she might never eat anything again. The panic was returning. 'But I'll sit in the car——'

'I insist that you come in with us. If you refuse, then of course I shall cancel the lunch.'

'Oh.' He meant it too. 'Then, if you put it like that, you don't give me a choice, do you? I can hardly see you and Denvers starve.'

'Precisely. You may eat as little as you want. I think, however, once you are inside, you may feel differently.'

And so it proved. The restaurant, a long, low ivy-covered building, was welcoming—and superbly fitted. There were only a few others lunching, and Polly had a shrewd idea that Boris Leander was not only known to them, but was highly regarded. They were ushered to a table in the corner, set for three. Polly had wondered, and was not even slightly surprised that Denvers was going to eat with them. One or two mildly interested faces turned in their direction as they sat down—and were averted as Boris Leander looked round the room, coolly, half smiling. Yet Polly shivered faintly at the look. It clearly told anyone concerned to get on with their food and mind their own business. The restaurant owner, as bursting with pride as the little mayor had been the previous day, attended to them personally.

The food was superb, but Polly was scarcely aware of what she ate. She ate enough to keep Boris Leander happy. Happy? She thought. That's hardly the word. Not in any way could Boris Leander's manners towards her be faulted. When they had eaten and were waiting for coffee and liqueurs to be served, she went to the ladies' room. As she returned, both Boris and Denvers stood, Boris to move her chair for her. 'Thank you,' she murmured.

'You have enjoyed your lunch?'

'Thank you, it was very nice.'

'Good. After we have finished coffee, we will leave. We should be home in two hours.'

She watched him as he went on to speak to the chauffeur about their route to Leander House. I wonder, she thought, what goes on in his mind? He is using me, I know that, and when his father dies, my job will be over, and I'll never see him again. I'll go back to the *Wallington Courier*, find a flat, and life will go on as before. And Boris Leander will remain a man of mystery. He has built a wall around himself that no one can penetrate, certainly not me. She opened her handbag to check she had her purse, and heard Boris's voice addressing her: 'I would like a few words with you, Polly, before we leave.' She saw that Denvers was standing, moving away, and she looked up at Boris.

'What about?'

'About what will happen when we arrive. Would you object to having your hair-style altered slightly?' This was something she had only briefly thought about.

She shrugged. 'It all depends. In what way?'

'Denvers' wife was a hairdresser before they married. She is already at Leander House. She will advise you. Nothing drastic, I assure you. Your hair is lovely as it is.'

She smiled. 'Thank you. It's rather curly—as I'm sure you've noticed. There's not a lot you can do with it.'

'I'm sure.' He put out his hand and swept her hair slightly off her forehead. His touch burned like fire. 'My wife had it swept off her forehead, so.' He took his hand away suddenly as if he too were aware of the fire.

'I don't mind,' she felt breathless, aware of him as a man. Just like that, in one second, there was an awareness that hurt. 'Will—will I meet your father today?'

'No. Better you rest, see Mrs Denvers, get settled in. Tomorrow is soon enough. Now, have you finished, Polly?'

'Yes, thank you.'

'Shall we go?'

'Yes, of course.' He lifted one hand, and the owner came over, face beaming yet anxious.

'Everything to your satisfaction, Mr Leander?'

'Perfectly, Charles. Thank you.' A bill was signed, a note changed hands, they were ushered out to the silently throbbing Daimler with Denvers at the wheel. Then they were on their way, on the final stage of the journey.

They reached Leander House at four. The house was hidden from the road by trees and a high wall of grey stone. It came into sight after a few minutes of slow driving, and Denvers slowed the car even further as if sensing Polly's gasp of wonder. She slid the window down and stared. 'What a beautiful house!' she whispered. It was large, grey stone, ivy-covered, long tall windows, gracious and elegant, facing them a few hundred yards away, surrounded by rich green lawns and trees, and with an air of quiet beauty that reached out to Polly and held her fascinated.

'Yes, it is,' Boris agreed quietly. 'It is my favourite home.'

That brought her down to earth. For how many more did he possess? She looked at him, smiled wryly.

'I suppose you have a few others tucked away somewhere,' she commented.

'Three. Did I sound as if I were bragging? I'm sorry, I didn't intend to.'

For some absurd reason she felt annoyed with him. Spikily she answered: 'Not at *all*. It's just that not everyone has a choice.' Her eyes sparked fire, and she saw an answering spark in his own. His voice was perfectly calm and steady as he answered:

'Now you are annoyed. Would you prefer me to pretend something I am not?'

'No. I know you're extremely rich—*everyone* does —why shouldn't you have several homes?'

'Why not indeed?' He smiled, but there was pain in that smile, and she wondered again about him. But only briefly, for they were drawing nearer, and the doors were opened wide by a tall dark woman who stood waiting on the step. She was dressed in black, and while her face held a smile of welcome, Polly, in a sudden flash of insight, was aware that this woman would not like her. But who was she? She hoped not Denvers' wife, for she liked him.

'Mrs Harris,' murmured Boris, as if in answer. 'She will take care of you.' I'll bet she will, thought Polly, heart sinking. Her instinct was confirmed as they walked up the steps to be greeted by the housekeeper.

'Welcome back, Mr Leander,' she said warmly, then looked at Polly. The eyes were like ice, the smile was cool. 'How d'you do, Miss Summers.'

'How d'you do,' Polly smiled back. Denvers drove the car away, and they went into the large wood-panelled hall, richly carpeted in red and gold with a staircase leading off to the first floor, and several doors either side.

'How is my father, Lena?' asked Boris.

'Much the same, sir. I prepared him for your arrival as you instructed, but I said nothing about——' Her eyes flickered to Polly, briefly.

'No, of course. Take Polly up to her room, will you? Denvers will bring her cases up afterwards.'

'Of course. This way, please, Miss Summers.' She

led the way up the wide staircase on to a further wider landing, again with doors off, and two corridors leading away to the wings of the house. Quietly Polly followed, feet silent on lush carpet, and Mrs Harris opened a door wide, and said: 'This is your room.'

Polly looked and gasped. She had been given what was clearly the best guest room. It was exquisitely furnished with a fourposter bed, covered with a white fur coverlet; an oyster grey carpet that seemed to go on for ever in the large room, and contemporary furniture in pale blonde wood that blended unobtrusively with everything else. A large vase of flowers on a centre table completed the picture of sheer luxury. Had Zoe been with her, Polly would have said an appreciate 'Wowee!' but she didn't think Mrs Harris would appreciate—or approve. She looked as though she disapproved of everything about Polly, who was by now beginning to feel as though she were dressed in all the wrong clothes.

'It's a lovely room,' she said lamely.

'It is indeed.' She was awarded a tight little smile. Mrs Harris's eyes were icy grey—and Polly noticed for the first time that she wasn't as old as she had at first thought. She was possibly in her late thirties. A faint suspicion stirred, and was gone. It was to return later that day. Mrs Harris was in fact a good-looking woman, face skilfully made up to emphasise good bone structure, high cheekbones and narrow chin.

'Your bathroom is beyond that mirrored door in the corner.' Mrs Harris pointed. 'The wardrobes should prove adequate, and you have your own television.'

She crossed the room, opened what appeared to be a fitted cupboard, and a large television set was revealed. 'And if you need anything, the bell push is at the side of your bed. Either I or Mrs Denvers will attend to you.'

'Oh, yes, I'd like to meet her.' Polly hoped the chauffeur's wife would prove to be more amenable than this woman. There was a definitely cold aura about her that made Polly feel uneasy.

'Then I'll send her up immediately. Dinner will be at seven, Miss Summers, if there's anything you want me for before that time, I shall be at your service.' She nodded briskly and walked out. Polly collapsed on the bed with a sigh of relief. The housekeeper's manners were as immaculate as her appearance. There were no words or gestures made to indicate her feelings and yet Polly felt a sense of strong antipathy flowing from her in almost tangible waves. It was new and unusual for Polly, whose easygoing friendliness made her popular wherever she went. And yet it was just a beginning, did Polly but know it.

She took off her shoes and wandered over to open the mirrored door in the wall. As she peeped into a luxuriously fitted pink-tiled bathroom, there came a tap on her door and it opened to reveal a woman so like Denvers that Polly exclaimed: 'You're Mrs Denvers, aren't you?'

'I am.' The woman's face broke into a smile.

'But you're like brother and sister!' Polly felt instant empathy with this woman.

'I know. Everyone says that.' She came in and held

out her hand. 'I'm very pleased to meet you. Tom told me——' she hesitated, looked round, then: 'My God, you're her double!'

Polly sat on the bed, patting the coverlet beside her. 'Sit down, please,' she begged. 'I'm still confused. All this has happened so suddenly, you see. One minute I'm at a reception to meet your boss, the next minute I'm being whisked up here and into this——' she held her arms out indicating the room. 'I need someone to just talk to me for a minute.'

'Okay. I'm here.' Mrs Denvers grinned at her. 'My name's Janet, by the way.'

'Polly. Tell me, Janet, am I really like her—Mr Leander's late wife, I mean?'

'Yes. It was a shock—walking in. I'm sure it'll work —I hope it does. I like old Mr Leander very much.' Tears filled her eyes and she blinked furiously. 'Take no notice of me. Aren't I stupid?'

'No, you're not. You've given me confidence, anyway. I've been getting butterflies ever since yesterday——'

'You don't need to. He's really too ill anyway to question you, but if he thinks you're Crystal, come back by some miracle, he'll die happy. And now, having seen you, he'll think the miracle has happened.'

Polly heaved a sigh. 'I hope so. Thanks anyway, Janet. Your Mrs Harris made me feel like a gauche teenager——'

'Oh, *her*! She's not *my* Mrs Harris, thank the lord. She rules the roost here though, and let's face it, does a first-class job. She nursed old Mr Leander through a bad illness some time back as well.'

'Oh.' Polly pulled a face. 'I'll be nicer to her. I just got the slight impression she didn't like me, and as she'd only just met me it threw me off balance.'

'Mmm, well, she wouldn't, would she?' Janet looked at her, a wealth of meaning in her voice.

Polly raised an enquiring eyebrow. 'Umm? Do you mean what I think you mean?'

'Probably.' Janet grinned. 'It's obvious to everyone else. She's crackers about Mr Leander.'

'But *Mr* Harris?'

'She's divorced—a free woman. And indispensable to Mr Leander—and his father. And Mr Leander is a very rich man.'

'I know. But surely she knows I'm only here for a——' Polly faltered slightly, 'a short while?'

'Yes. But she knews how much Mr Leander adored his wife. And she's got eyes. She's seen how much like her you are. Put yourself in her place. He's never even looked at another woman since the plane crash —I'm sorry, I shouldn't be talking like this, Polly. Tom would be furious if he knew——'

'I'm sorry too. But of course you're right. We'll change the subject. I've no right to pry at all. But one thing—you're going to help me with my hair, aren't you?'

'Yes. And·we *can* talk about that. I used to be a hair-dresser, so I do know what I'm doing. That's just to reassure you. We'll discuss it later, after dinner. Mr

Leander will be busy, I've got all evening to spare, so if you like, I'll come up here with all my stuff and we'll decide what we're going to do.'

'Fine. Dinner's not till seven. What do I do till then?'

'Anything you like. Shall I show you round the house and grounds?'

'Lovely. I hoped you'd offer. Er—it won't get you into trouble with Mrs H if you do?'

Janet smiled. 'She's not in any position to tell me what to do. Mr Leander's instructions are that I'm to help you in every way—and now I've met you, that suits me fine.'

There was a tap on the door and Janet opened it. Tom stood there with Polly's cases. 'Come in, love. Want me to help you unpack?' Janet said.

'No, I'll manage, thanks.' Polly grimaced. 'I'm not even sure I want to unpack my meagre selection now I've come here——'

'Never mind that. You look fine to me. Got any long dresses?'

'I brought two.'

'Well, he changes for dinner normally. And if you like I'll run up one for you—I've bags of material and patterns. I do all the sewing round here.'

'Thanks. I'll take you up on that if I may.'

Tom spoke: 'Would you like to see round the place, Miss Summers? Mr Leander said you're to do exactly as you wish——'

'We've already fixed it up,' his wife answered. 'Tell

you what, I'll let you have a wash, and come back in, say, fifteen minutes? Is that all right?'

'Fine.' Polly smiled at them both. 'I still feel a bit strange, but if you help me settle in, I'll feel much more at home. Oh, that reminds me—I promised to phone home when I arrived. Is there one handy?'

'You have your own phone here.' Tom crossed the room and drew back the curtains to reveal a white telephone at the end of the wide windowseat. 'It's an internal one, but if you need an outside line you switch this gadget at the bottom to the far right, see?' he demonstrated. 'The other switches are for various parts of the house. I don't imagine you'll need them, though.'

'Thanks.' As they made for the door, Polly added: 'See you in a quarter of an hour.'

They were gone. She was alone. She looked round her, absorbing the atmosphere, then went over to the telephone, picked up the receiver, and began to dial Zoe's number.

She had seen round the house and gardens, and, overwhelmed by it all, lay on her bed before changing for dinner. The impressions whirled, kaleidoscope fashion, around her mind as she tried to assimilate them all to pass on to Zoe. The large library, drawing room, dining room and conservatory crammed with colourful hothouse plants from all over the world. The house was luxury personified—not ostentatious, but beautiful. Yet it lacked something essential that had puzzled Polly at first until, entering the last room, she had realised. That last room had been a sun lounge at the side of the house, a long narrow, extremely comfortable room with yellow scatter rugs, a bookcase, floor-length windows that opened on to a stone patio with trellised walls and roses climbing, and large pots of geraniums blazing scarlet in the sun. 'This was designed by Mr Leander's father a few years back,' Janet told her.

'It's lovely——' She could almost sense the love that had gone into the planning—and it was then she knew what lacked in the rest of the house. Beautiful it might be, but it was empty of warmth. Not in a physical sense, but empty of emotion, as though it was not a home, merely a house, a beautiful shell. In a way, it was like Boris Leander himself. She waited to meet his father, someone who had clearly put his mark on the house, or part of it.

Was it perhaps because some light had gone from the place when Crystal was killed? It seemed probable, but it was something Polly couldn't ask anyone. It was time to prepare for dinner. Seven, he had said. She had not see Boris Leander since he had left her in the hall. Doubtless he was a busy man. At least she knew where the dining room was, and she would be there on the dot of seven. She checked her watch with the electric alarm clock by her bedside. Half an hour to go. Enough time for a shower, change and make up. She wondered if he would turn up for dinner. She had no idea of the kind of lives that business tycoons led, but was as well aware as anyone else that they would be busy. He had to eat. She worked on the premise that she would see him at the meal, and went to run her shower. She wanted to look her best.

A final look in the long mirror, a rebellious curl tucked back into place, and Polly was ready. Her dress was a blue flowered cotton, very simple, and it made her look about eighteen. She rarely wore make-up, save a little lipstick and eyeshadow, but this evening had put on as well a light foundation, eyeliner and a touch of blusher. The effect was pleasing, and it gave her the touch of confidence she needed. Normally well-adjusted and happy, Polly was still feeling too strange in her new environment to relax. Boris Leander, how-ever courteous, was formidable. There was no other way to describe him. And she had not forgotten the ice on Mrs Harris's face.

She picked up her bag, and found her way down the stairs into the magnificent hall. The door to the dining room was open, and after taking a deep breath, Polly went in. Boris Leander turned slowly from the window to face her. He held a silver goblet in his hand, and he wore a grey mohair suit, crisp white shirt, grey tie. His dark-tanned face was serious—then he smiled. 'Hello, Polly,' he said. 'I hope you have settled in well?'

'Yes, thanks.' She stood by the table, hand resting on the back of the tall chair at one end.

'Would you like some sherry—or an aperitif?'

'Dubonnet and soda if you have it.'

'Certainly. Do sit down. We dine alone tonight. I thought it would be an opportunity to talk about tomorrow. Janet tells me you have already spoken?'

'Yes. She showed me round the house and gardens. She's being very kind.'

He handed her a large silver goblet and held the chair as she sat down. Then he sat in the chair opposite, at the end of the table. 'Dinner won't be a moment. She and Denvers will take you out in the car any time you wish to do any shopping. We aren't far from Carlisle, and just an hour's drive from Edinburgh. While you are here my car is at your disposal.' He spoke in a kindly manner, yet remote, as if his thoughts were far away. Polly watched him stroke the stem of his goblet absentmindedly.

'I suppose you're very busy?'

He looked across at her. His eyes were very direct, cool and hard, that unusual green that made her feel as if he could see straight through her—through everybody with whom he came into contact. 'Yes, I usually am,' he agreed. 'But I have arranged my affairs over the next few——' he hesitated slightly—'weeks so as to spend as much time as possible here.'

'I see. Have you mentioned me to your—father—yet?' she stopped, not sure how to continue. The sensation of strangeness was returning. She took a deep swallow of the sharp, bitter-sweet aperitif.

'That is what I want to speak to you about. His comprehension is very limited, yet I think I have prepared him sufficiently. He is well sedated constantly, and has two nurses in round-the-clock attendance. He is in the west wing of the house, by the way, the part you did not visit. A doctor calls every day. I have already telephoned him, and the nurses have been briefed. So all is ready for you in the morning.'

She swallowed hard. 'At what time?'

'After breakfast, about nine-thirty. Time means nothing to him——' for a moment, she saw pain cross his features, swiftly controlled and banished. 'I pray this will succeed.'

'So do I,' Polly murmured. She raised her goblet. 'I won't let you down.'

A brief smile. 'I know.'

And for a moment, something reached out between them, and touched them, and Polly experienced a sensation of warmth, and caught a glimpse of the man he really was, and her heart bumped violently. Then she saw that he was aware of this something too, for his face changed, and he looked at her. He was about to say something when the door opened and Mrs Harris came in with a maid, carrying soup. The moment was lost. Polly wondered what he had been about to say. Perhaps she would never know.

CHAPTER FOUR

SHE lay awake that night for ages, until at last she got out of bed and sat down on the window seat, looking out of the darkened gardens, shadow-filled and mysteriously beautiful. In the distance an owl hooted, and was answered, then silence again. A thin pale moon silvered the tops of the trees, and the air through the open window was faintly perfumed and very sharp and cold. Polly shivered briefly.

All was quiet in the house. It was past midnight. A faint elusive scent was added to that of the sleeping flowers, and she sniffed, looked, caught the red glow from outside, and saw the dark shadowy figure standing nearby. As her eyes became accustomed to the darkness the figure became clearer. Boris Leander was outside, smoking a cigar. The red dot arced to the ground and vanished, then he walked on, soft-footed in the dark, and she heard a door click shut. So he too was finding sleep elusive. Unless he always took a walk before bedtime. He had told her during the course of the meal that he needed very little sleep, and was often up at five for a swim in the pool. She had seen it on her walk round the gardens with Janet, a large, kidney-shaped swimming pool with lounging chairs and several changing cabins. She could see it from her window in daylight, partially hidden by trees but quite close to the house. When she had smilingly said that she hadn't brought her swimsuit he had told her there was a selection of new ones, and Janet would let her have one any time.

The question of money had also been raised. Polly recalled the conversation now as she sat hugging her knee on the wide seat. She always found discussions of money embarrassing. She earned an adequate salary at the *Wallington Courier*, and had a little saved in the bank, and she managed comfortably. Boris Leander, as if sensing this, didn't press the point of what he would give her for her stay at Leander House, for which she had been much relieved, but she had the uncomfortable idea that he intended, all the same, to give her a large amount. She leaned her head on the cool hard windowpane, remembering his face as he had spoken. She could see every detail of his features etched with clarity in her mind's eye, the high cheekbones, square strong chin, mobile mouth, straight nose—the eyes. They were somehow both the most fascinating and most disturbing feature about him. His eyes hid his secrets well, and yet somehow when he looked at her it was as if he saw everything. She closed her own eyes as if in silent protest, and her whole body tingled at the memory of the something she had glimpsed briefly, just before dinner, when his face had changed with an awareness that was almost frightening. What had it been? She didn't know—and yet, strangely, there was an awareness in her as well of what might happen again. How soon she did not know, but the certainty was there.

It was no use; she knew she would not sleep. She was wide awake as she had been during the afternoon. Boris had told her during dinner that if ever she needed anything at all, day or night, she had only to press the bell by her bedside, but she had no intention of doing so. Polly was most definitely not used to being waited on. She knew where the kitchens were: down the corridor, down the stairs, and along to the back of the house. She would go down, heat some milk and bring it back up to drink. If Boris Leander were still about it wouldn't matter. Polly's cotton dressing gown was highly respectable, buttoned from neck to hem, and she was thirsty. In any case, he would probably be in his study—the one room in the main house that Janet had not taken her in, merely indicated the door, and told her that the room was totally private. No one entered save a trusted cleaner briefly every morning to vacuum and dust. The secrecy of it fascinated Polly as she had visualised what might lie inside. Computers? Rows of phones? Filing cabinets? Her imagination was vivid—and Ed would probably give a year's salary for the briefest glimpse inside. She smiled to herself at the thought, put on her dressing gown and buttoned it, every single button, from neck to toes.

Dim lights burned along the passage, and in the hall, and downstairs a solitary lamp cast a soft glow, guiding her towards the kitchens. A thin sliver of gold light came from under Boris Leander's study door, and she crept past as silent as any ghost, found the kitchen door, and opened it. The fluorescent light flooded the room, dazzling her, and she blinked. Everything gleamed, new pin clean, totally immaculate. It seemed an impertinence to disturb anything there, but Polly now longed so much for warm milk that nothing else mattered. She would replace everything where she found it. She took a pan from a cupboard, opened the refrigerator door to see seven pints of milk in the door shelf. Something else caught her eye as well, the remains of a strawberry cheesecake on a plate, and her stomach gave a brief rumble of protest. It had been quite delicious. Weakly she looked at it, then, muttering: 'No!' took out a bottle of milk and closed the door.

While the milk heated she found a tall beaker and waited, tapping her foot, refusing to think of cheesecake—thinking of daffodils, of swimming pools instead. Thinking of cheesecake——

The door opened softly and she turned guiltily. Boris Leander stood there watching her. 'Oh!' she gasped. 'I'm sorry——' she rescued the pan in the nick of time.

'Sorry?' He walked soft-footed towards her. For a moment a smile touched his mouth briefly, then was gone. 'Please don't apologise. Is that what you needed? Some warm milk?'

'I couldn't sleep.' She felt oddly on the defensive. 'This always helps me.'

'Then perhaps I shall have some too.' He took the

milk and poured some more into the pan she had just emptied. 'Do you mind if I join you?'

'Of course not.' He replaced the bottle in the refrigerator and lifted out the plate of cheesecake. 'I've just realised I'm hungry too. Would you like a piece?'

'Oh!' she groaned. 'I was looking before—but I daren't——'

'Sit down. I'll get two plates.' He still wore the grey suit, but had removed his tie, unbuttoned the top of his shirt, revealing the darkness of hair at the base of his throat. He sat down at the table and cut two pieces of cake, handing her one on a plate with a fork. 'Hell!' he jumped to his feet as the forgotten milk boiled over with a fine splutter, dowsing the gas. Polly couldn't help it. She began to laugh, and after a brief startled look at her, Boris Leander joined it.

'Oh—I'm sorry——' she jumped to her feet and fetched a dishcloth from the sink and began to wipe round the gas ring. She was still laughing, and he was oh, so different now. He was human.

'Please don't do that,' he said. 'Leave it——'

'No. It dries horribly if you do.' She turned to him; he was beside her, looking down at her, reaching out for the dishcloth in polite protest at her actions, and for a moment their hands touched.

That was the moment Mrs Harris chose to walk in. There was a brief electric silence, Polly turned in dismay, and Boris Leander looked across at her. Polly saw the housekeeper's face in the moment before the mask was replaced. 'I'm sorry, sir,' she said. 'I heard noises and thought——' she sounded momentarily confused. She wore a long deep blue housecoat that fitted her slim figure to perfection, and her hair, which Polly had only seen swept off her face in a neat chignon, was loose and flowing round her shoulders.

'That's all right, Lena,' he said, 'everything's under control. Miss Summers and I are having a late supper. We'll clear up after ourselves.'

'Allow me, sir.' She swept forward, her walk gracious and controlled, and Polly thought with a start of shock: she's furious. She also knew why. Lena Harris took the dishcloth from Polly and began wiping away at the cooker top, and Boris Leander's voice cut in, very quietly, but with an edge of ice:

'You can go back to bed. I'll do that.' The woman paused, froze, then:

'Of course. Goodnight.' She turned, and went out, closing the door behind her. Polly went to the table and sat down.

'Oh, dear,' she said softly.

Boris looked at her. 'That sounds rather sad,' he remarked, refilling the pan. She looked up at him, and smiled reluctantly. But she said nothing, for what was there to say? *She doesn't like me*—and she certainly doesn't like me having cosy supper parties in her kitchen with *you*?

He nodded, as if there were no need for words. 'Mrs Harris is very—conscientious,' he said, as if he had chosen the word carefully.

'Yes,' said Polly.

The milk safely heated without further disaster, he sat down, and looked at Polly. 'And you are very astute,' he commented. He touched her plate. 'Eat your cheesecake.'

'I know she doesn't like me, if that's what you mean,' she retorted, stung by something in his voice to unusual frankness.

He raised one eyebrow and a corner of his wide mouth twitched. 'Really? What makes you say that?'

And suddenly it was there again, that something that had reached out to touch them both before, filling the room with a simmering undercurrent of tension that made Polly's skin prickle. They were alone, a man and a woman, late at night, and the barriers were down. Their lives were a world apart, but because of an accident of looks, and an illness, they were together in this house, met by chance, and only briefly. Polly took a deep breath, because she had never met a man like this before.

'A woman's instinct,' she answered. She looked directly at him, her eyes wide and clear, with the brightness of her youth. 'But I can live with it.'

He nodded, as if in acknowledgement of something deeper than her words.

'You are my guest,' he said softly, 'as well as having come here to do me a great service. Which means that while you are here, for whatever length of time that may be, you will be treated with the utmost courtesy by all my staff.' It was most strange. The conversation was on one level, the words normal, yet it went deeper than that by far, and they both knew it. Something linked them, and because of it, nothing would ever be quite the same again. It was as if, briefly, the world had tilted out of balance. 'I hope I make myself clear.'

'Yes, you do.' She laid her hand on the table, and she knew what he was going to do, as clearly as if he had said it. He put his hand gently on top of hers—a large strong hand, the back covered with dark hair, a tanned hand that covered hers completely.

'If anything bothers you, anything at all, you are to tell me.'

'I will.' He took his hand away; the touch had been very disturbing. He drank his milk, Polly drank hers, and toyed with the cheesecake, because for some reason she was no longer hungry. She only knew she didn't want the evening to end.

'Are you feeling tired yet?' he asked. If he wasn't a mind-reader, he was something very near it.

'No, I'm afraid not. But don't worry—I'll be awake in the morning at the right time.'

He smiled. 'I can get you a sleeping pill from the nurse if you like.'

Her eyes widened in horror. 'Oh, no—I mean, no, thanks. I'd be frightened to take one.'

'Don't look alarmed. You're very lucky you don't ever need them.'

'Do you?'

'No. But I live in the kind of high-powered world where the people I deal with are generally under the influence of some kind of pep pill or tranquilliser—I avoid anything like that. I've seen what they can do.'

'I should think you're strong enough in yourself not to need any outside help,' she said, surprising herself. The barriers were well and truly down.

A brief smile. 'Is that how I strike you?'

'Yes. Aren't you? Strong, I mean?'

'I've never thought about it.'

'Then you should look in a mirror some time.'

He laughed. 'I've been looking in a mirror every morning for the past twenty years,' he stroked his chin reflectively, 'ever since I started shaving—and all I see is the same old features—nothing special, I assure you.'

Polly suddenly realised that he meant it. He had none of that smug awareness carried by the man who knows he is strong and handsome. She wondered about him, deeply wanted to know all there was to know about him. It was said he had never looked at a woman since his wife died—but it surely could not be entirely true. She felt warmth spread through her at the implication of her own thoughts, and was terrified he would guess them. Yet she couldn't think of a thing to say. It was as if her mind had locked in her confusion.

He stood up, took beakers and plates to the sink, and ran the tap. She followed. 'You wash, I'll dry,' she said, released by his movement.

'Right.' She was terribly aware of him beside her at the sink, aware of his height, the power she sensed, the sheer maleness of him. She could imagine him making love——

She dropped the plate, and it shattered on the tiled floor. 'My God!' She looked at it in shocked dismay and bent to pick up the pieces. 'I'm so sorry——' she began.

'For a plate? Ah—leave those pieces, you'll cut yourself. I'll get a——' But it was too late. She already had. The blood welled up from her thumb where a shard of pottery had sliced it as she touched.

He put his hands on her arms, pulled her up, and looked at her. Then he took her hand and put her thumb under the cold tap. 'Stay *still*,' he commanded. 'And don't *move*. You are quite definitely a menace to society.' As she opened her mouth, he added: 'And don't apologise again. I am a man of infinite patience, but——' and he grinned at her and walked away.

Polly did exactly as she was told, watched him return with a first-aid box, and one minute later had a neatly bandaged thumb. 'Let's go,' he said. 'I fear for my safety if we stay here any longer.' He put his hand lightly on her elbow. 'This way.'

'Where are you taking me?'

'You'll see. I have the solution to your insomnia— and also a cure for the shock you are undoubtedly suffering after cutting yourself.'

'But I'm not——' she began.

'Don't argue. You may be my guest, but there are times when the host has to make snap decisions. This way.' He led her out of the kitchen—and she knew where he was taking her. He opened his study door and ushered her in.

Whatever she had expected, it was not this. Not this comfortable, lived-in, man's room with deep settee and chairs in brown leather, made to be lounged in—and only one large desk by the window, with two telephones to justify its title of 'study'.

'Oh,' she said. 'I thought——'

Boris had closed the door. 'What did you think?' he sounded amused.

'Janet said it was your study—and very private.'

'True. It is also my den, the room where I relax, put my feet up, read a book, and know I can be left entirely and completely alone. I have lights on the phone which I can ignore if I don't wish to answer. You are only the second guest who has ever been in here. Please sit down, I'm going to get you a brandy—strictly for medicinal purposes, I assure you.'

Now that she was in, and able to take it all in properly, she could see the cupboards lining the walls, not modern ones, but in keeping with the character of the room. She could understand it then, his need for privacy, the knowledge that here alone he could truly relax. The settee was extremely comfortable. She sat back and sank into soft cool leather and gave an appreciative 'mmm'.

He handed her a glass. 'How's the thumb?'

She had forgotten it. 'Oh, fine. I think the brandy will complete the cure.'

'I'm sure it will.' He sat down at the other end of the settee, a respectable distance between them. 'Your health.'

'And yours.' She sipped the smooth mellow cognac, and immediately felt a warm glow spread through her system.

'Do you mind if I smoke a cigar?'

'Mind? Of course not. This is your room.'

'But if it bothers you——'

'It doesn't. I smelt cigar smoke before, when I couldn't sleep. I'd gone to sit at the window and I saw you walking outside.'

'Taking a last stroll before bed. I usually do that. I must warn you, by the way, not to go outside after dark on your own. We have two alsatians which are allowed to roam freely at night, and unless they know you——' he paused, and lit a thin cigar.

'You don't need to tell me. I get the picture,' she said hastily. 'But in winter—do they live out of doors?' Polly liked animals.

He smiled. 'They are working dogs, not household pets—but I assure you I treat them well. You passed the stables on your tour?'

'Yes, but——'

'My head gardener and his wife have a flat over there, and the dogs stay with them during the day. At night they are taken down and the stable door is left open. Inside are two kennels. They sleep there, but if anyone moved near the house they would be out investigating, I assure you. So you see, Polly, they are well looked after.'

She felt herself flush, as if she had accused him of neglect, and he smiled. 'I can read your mind,' he said.

'You must learn to hide your feelings more skilfully.'

'As you do?' She felt her skin tingle on her neck as she said it, but couldn't have stopped it coming out if she had tried.

'Perhaps.' His eyes were very level on her, very hard, drawing out her mind, touching her with his power. 'Is that how I seem?'

'Yes. You have a wall round you—a remoteness——' she stopped. 'I'm very sorry, I shouldn't have said that——'

'Why not? I asked. It is interesting. Not many people speak as frankly to me as you do.'

'Perhaps because they're frightened to.'

'Oh, very possibly. Which is why it is a refreshing change to have someone speak their mind.'

'But you wouldn't like it to happen all the time.'

'What makes you say that?'

'Because you're used to your power. You must be. You are immensely wealthy, and wealth, whether you like it or not, brings its own power. I may be a refreshing change as you put it, but I'm only here for a while, and I'm not dependent on you in any way. Your wealth impresses me only insofar as it must impress any normal human being——' she stopped again, and looked accusingly at her brandy glass, then at him. 'I'm talking too much.' She said it with finality.

His mouth twisted. 'Then have some more brandy.'

'Thank you no. I seem to have had more than enough.'

'I think I will.' He uncurled himself from the settee,

and refilled his glass. 'Do you wish to go to bed yet?'

'In a few minutes. I'm feeling rather tired now, to be quite honest.' She put her head back on the arm of the settee and looked up at the ceiling. 'Just one question I must ask before morning. What do I call your father?'

'My—wife—always called him Poppa. It was a little joke between them——' his voice was almost hesitant, as if the words had the power, even after that time, to recall memories that were painful. 'She was—American.'

'I see.' She repeated the word softly. 'Poppa. Is that right? I—er—can't do an American accent.'

'No matter. She had lost the accent anyway, only a trace remained. Just be—all you need is to sit—not talk much——'

'Please, on the first visit, will you stay with me?'

'Of course. It will only be for a short time anyway, then afterwards, depending on how it goes, you'll stay a little longer on each visit. But I shall be there, or within hearing distance, if you wish it, I promise you.' He added softly, 'It won't be for long. The doctors have assured me——' he stopped. Instinctively Polly reached her hand out to touch his.

'Please,' she said. Her voice broke, tears filled her eyes. 'You don't need to say——' she couldn't go on. 'I'd better go.' She rose to her feet and put the glass down on a table. Boris Leander stood, took hold of her and turned her to face him, looked at her for a few heart-stopping seconds, then, very gently, pulled her towards him. He held her closely against his breast, and she could feel the deeply steady heartbeat, feel the strength of his arms around her, and knew an intense surge of warmth filling her whole body with an exquisite agony of sweetness.

'Don't upset yourself,' he said, his voice a murmur against her ear, his breath in her hair. 'It has all been said, and thought out. You must not cry.'

'I'm not crying for me,' she whispered. 'Don't you see, it's——' she looked up at him, eyes glistening, face gentle with concern and tiredness—and with that indefinable something that his nearness did to her. 'I care, that's all. I *care*.'

And inevitably, with a slow gentle movement neither were able to resist, as inexorably as the seconds ticking past on a clock, his face came closer, until it blurred with her tears, and his lips were on hers, warm, firm, sensuously moving, stirring a response in her that frightened and excited her all at the same time, and she thought she would faint or die, because no man had ever kissed her in such a way before. She had been kissed many times, some casual, end-of-party kisses, some more serious, some utterly delightful—and she had enjoyed most, if not all, some more than others.

But this, now, was so different that it was as if she had never known a man's lips before. She was drowned in the sea of her senses, lost in the other world of emotion, which knew no reason or sense, only the now —and the kiss—and there was nothing else save that.

'My God!' He held her away from him, and looked down at her, eyes so dark they looked nearly

black, his face shadowed with the light behind him.
'I had no right to do that——'

Polly wrenched herself free, before he could see what
must lie revealed on her own face, turned away, whispered: 'I must go——' And before he could move she
reached the door and, opening it, ran out.

At half past seven Janet brought her a cup of tea. Polly
surfaced from a sound sleep, mind totally blank as
yet—then remembered.

She yawned and patted the cover of the bed. 'Morning, Janet. You are kind. That's just what I need to
wake me. I've slept like a log.'

Janet sat on the edge of the bed. 'You can have
breakfast in bed if you like.'

'Can I really? What a lovely thought. No, better not.
I mustn't get spoiled. Is Mr Leander up?'

'Yes, I passed him on the way up. He says to tell
you he'll see you about nine-thirty. He was going to
make a few phone calls to Australia and New Zealand
—this is the best time to phone them.'

'Good heavens, is it? I must remember that.' Polly
grinned at her. She felt remarkably well, considering
everything. She felt splendid. She touched her new
hair-style, done by Janet the previous evening after
dinner and before her midnight journey to the kitchen.
The rebellious curl had been somehow smoothed; the
difference was only slight, yet it gave Polly an added
confidence for what could prove a difficult task ahead.
'You did a good job on these tangles of mine. Thanks.'

'A pleasure, any time. I'll go now, as long as you're sure you won't have breakfast up here—and Polly, good luck. I'll be thinking of you later.'

'Thanks. I'll see you before lunch, will I?'

'Yes.' Janet stood up. 'Drink your tea. You'll be breakfasting alone. Mr Leander had his at seven. Oh, and be nice to Mrs Harris. She doesn't seem in too sunny a mood this morning.' She pulled a face.

Polly laughed. 'I *wonder* why?'

Janet narrowed her eyes. 'You *know*?'

Polly shrugged. 'I'd gone down to warm some milk because I couldn't sleep last night, and Boris came in the kitchen, so we had milk and cheesecake together. She came in, that's all.'

Janet grinned. 'Oh, boy, wait till I tell Tom!' she chuckled. 'Poor Lena, she wouldn't like that very much. She's not used to having her kitchen invaded for one thing, and for another—she's not used to women visitors.'

'I'll keep out of it in future,' Polly promised her. 'If looks could have killed——'

'Yes. Never mind, she won't dare say anything to you. We've had a little lecture about looking after you. She knows which side her bread's buttered on, if you'll pardon the slight pun. See you. Fingers crossed.' She did so, and went out. Polly thought about Lena Harris for a moment or two, then drank her tea and got out of bed.

She sat in the dining room and Boris Leander walked in. 'Good morning, Polly,' he said.

'Good morning.'

'Mind if I join you for a coffee?'

'Of course not.' He poured out two cups, and Polly helped herself to bacon and eggs from the heated dish on the table. 'I thought you were phoning Australia— Janet said.'

'I was. I heard you come down and decided I needed a break. And to tell you—please don't think of this visit to my father as anything of an ordeal. He is so ill he may not even recognise you—or rather the woman you are supposed to be.'

No mention of any kiss. It might never have happened. Perhaps it hadn't! Maybe I imagined it, she thought. But she knew she hadn't. There was no way that imagination, however vivid, could encompass that experience. Polly resolutely buttered herself a piece of toast and thanked Boris for her coffee. 'Is it all right if I go for a walk round the garden before we see your father?'

'Of course. Go anywhere you please. The alsatians accept people in the daytime. It is only after dark they become protective.'

'I see.' She laughed. 'I'll remember that. Is there anything you should tell me before we go?'

'No. Only that I shall address you as Crystal.'

'Of course. And you'll stay?'

'Yes.' He rubbed his forehead, as if tired. Quite suddenly Polly sensed that it was he who needed reassurance, not her. Just now, in this, he was not, for once, the powerful, dynamic man he always appeared.

She said quietly: 'It will be all right. I know it will. We're doing the right thing.'

CHAPTER FIVE

HER own words echoed round in her mind as she took her solitary walk. If only, now, she were so sure! She would soon find out. It was nearly nine, time to return to the house. She made her way back along the crazy paving in a walled garden some distance from the house itself, and breathed deeply, willing herself to feel and look calm. Boris Leander had gone out of the dining room and returned a minute later with a bottle of perfume. He had handed it to her. 'I nearly forgot this,' he said. 'Will you do me the favour of wearing some? It was—my wife's favourite perfume.' She had taken it to her room, and now she was going to put some on. Her hands were clammy with perspiration born of fear. Somehow that had seemed the most definite act of all—the putting on of another woman's favourite scent. He had bought it, he told her, the morning after meeting her, when they had decided, and she had agreed, to go back to Leander House with him. Putting it on would be the final commitment.

She ran up the steps, and into the house. All was quiet. Very slowly she walked up to her room and opened the bottle. She looked at it for a moment and the dreadful irony of it struck her like a blow to the heart. The perfume was by Worth: 'Je Reviens.' 'I will return.' Polly sat down on the bed, legs weak, and she wanted to cry.

There was a knock on her door, she answered something, she knew not what, and he walked in. Taking a deep breath, she dabbed the scent on her pulse points at throat and wrists. 'I'm ready,' she said.

The room was shaded, the white blinds fully drawn down. She remembered she had seen the windows from her walk in the garden, and wondered. Now she knew. The nurse who was sitting at the bedside of the gravely ill man rose as they went in, murmured: 'Good morning, sir,' nodded pleasantly to Polly, and went quietly out. As she left Boris Leander told her quietly:

'We will not stay long.' Polly trembled, then gathering all her courage, walked slowly to the bed, and took the man's hand.

'Hello, Poppa,' she whispered, and sat down on the chair beside the bed. He was a white shadow against the pillow, a mere shape in the bed. She felt the slightest squeeze, heard, in the merest breath of sound the words:

'Cry—stal—is you?'

'Yes, it's me. I'm home, Poppa, rest now. I'm here to stay.' Help me, she prayed, help me to get it right. She was rewarded by a sigh, a deep contented sigh.

For the next fifteen minutes she held the man's hand, and he stirred slightly once or twice, but that was all. He appeared to have fallen asleep. When Boris touched her lightly on the shoulder, she turned to look at him. He bent over his father.

'We have to leave now, Father,' he said softly. 'But we'll return later when you've rested.'

There seemed to be no response, then a sound, so faint at first she was not sure if she had heard. She leaned forward to catch any words, and heard:

'Come, later.'

'Yes, I promise.' She kissed his forehead. 'Rest now.' She carefully released her hand and laid his on the bed. Then, with Boris's hand on her arm to steady her, she went out of the room. The nurse went in as they left.

Outside in the corridor she turned, white-faced, to Boris. 'Was I all right?'

'Perfect. You could do no more.' He kept his hand on her arm as they walked back to the main part of the house. 'You need a coffee—or something stronger?'

'A coffee will do.'

'Will you go back after lunch?'

'I'll go back whenever you want. I didn't realise how ill he was. I'm sorry.'

'I know. I don't think it will be long now. A week—perhaps two—no one knows. He has a very strong will, he's a fighter. The doctor says it's a miracle he's still alive. But you did him good.'

'How could you tell?'

'He's rarely said more than one word at a time. He knew you—or thought he did.'

'And the doctor was agreeable?'

'How could he be otherwise? There is no hope. Anything that can ease his last days—that is all I ask.'

Polly was silenced. They reached the drawing room, and Boris pressed the bell by the fireplace and sat down on the long settee beside Polly. 'My morning is busy now. I shall have to leave you after we have drunk coffee. Would you like Janet and Tom to take you out anywhere? Say to the shops?'

'I don't know.' Her mind was still in a turmoil after that first meeting. The first hurdle taken—what next? That had been the most difficult. 'I'd like to get out for a while if you don't mind. But won't you need the car?'

'I have others.' He smiled. 'If I need to, I'll drive myself.' Mrs Harris came in at that moment, and he added, 'We'd like coffee, please, Lena.'

'Yes, sir.' She hesitated, seemed about to ask something, then went quietly out. Polly sat back and looked towards the window, but she saw only the grey face on the pillows, a face whose eyes had looked briefly at her. She would have sworn that.

'I'll stay longer this afternoon if you want,' she said. 'And you don't have to stay, not if you don't want to. Now I've met him I know——' she paused.

'Yes?' he prompted.

'I know I can—manage. But I wouldn't want to tire him. You'd have to tell the nurse to say when I've been there long enough.'

'I shall do that. You are very kind.'

She turned to face him. 'It's what I'm here for,' she said simply.

'And I know now that you will be a great comfort to him.'

'Then if you don't mind, I will do some shopping this morning. I've several odds and ends I need, and I don't think I'll be going out again.'

He stood up and walked away from her towards the window. She watched him go, a tall broad-shouldered man, filled with power—and just at that moment, with something else, indefinable. When he turned as he reached the window, she knew what it was. It was pain.

'Do I understand you right?'

'I'm not sure what you're thinking.' She stood up and walked slowly towards him. 'But I'll tell you what I mean. I will be with your father all the time I can, that's all. That's why I probably won't go out again.' She looked up at him, and it was all there, in her eyes, and she smiled.

Boris closed his eyes. 'Dear God,' he whispered. And Mrs Harris walked in with a silver tray and stood inside the door. Polly half turned at her entrance, and without thinking, said:

'Put it on the table, Mrs Harris, please.' She was hardly aware of giving an order. It seemed sensible—and she didn't like the way she stood, as if intending to stay. The housekeeper moved forward, her face an expressionless mask, put the tray down and said:

'Will that be all, Mr Leander?' Ice and fire mingled. The air was explosive. Boris appeared not to notice. He waved a dismissive hand.

'Yes, thank you.'

She turned and swept out. As if she hadn't even been in the room, he said to Polly: 'I don't know the words to thank you.'

'Then don't try. I'll pour out the coffee.' She left him standing there and returned to the table. On the tray was a silver coffee pot, milk jug and sugar bowl, two cups and saucers and a plate of chocolate mints and dainty petits fours. Polly looked at the closed door. She knew she had made an enemy, but at that moment, she didn't care.

She sat with Boris's father that afternoon for nearly two hours. During that time when there were just the two of them in the room, she held his hand and talked softly at times, at others was silent. She talked about the gardens, of the squirrel she had seen that morning, and the hedgehogs crossing the lawn, and of the flowers that were in bloom, and how they would see them together when he was better; whether he listened or heard, she didn't know, but she sensed his awareness, and just occasionally she felt a slight almost imperceptible squeeze of his hand on hers, and it seemed to her that she was, somehow, getting through to him.

She was tired, and it was Boris who came in at the end of the two hours and said: 'You must leave now, my dear. You will tire yourself.'

My dear, he had called her. For his father's benefit, but the words were a caress to her senses. Polly looked up at him. 'I have to go now, Poppa,' she whispered. 'I'll come again this evening. Would you like that?'

This time the squeeze on her hand was more definite. She leaned to kiss him, watched as Boris bent over to do the same, and the nurse came back into the room.

In the corridor she swayed slightly and he caught her arm. 'Polly, what is it?'

'Nothing, really. Just tiredness, that's all. I'll go to bed early tonight, I think.'

'Of course. Any books you wish to read? Anything you need?'

'No. I'll watch television—there's a good film on. May I make a phone call home?'

'You do not need to ask that. My home is yours while you are here.'

'But it's long-distance——'

'So? If you talk an hour, two hours, do you really think I would mind?'

'Well, no—but——' she shrugged and turned a helpless face towards him. 'You don't *understand*. It's *your* house. I'm a guest—I can't make free with your possessions——'

'But I have already said you must do just that. I can never repay what you are doing for my father. I know he is happier, I sense it already. I know him so well, and you don't. There is already a change in him; intangible, but *there*. He is easier in his mind.'

There was a question she had to ask him, and now seemed the time. 'Boris,' she said, 'I hope I'm not being impertinent, but why is your father so close to Crystal?

She was, after all, not his daughter, but his daughter-in-law.'

'Did I not explain? My wife is—was—the adopted daughter of my uncle, my father's brother. My uncle died several years ago, and my father looked after Crystal with my mother, when she was alive. They have always been very close.'

The next, inevitable question seemed to come out of its own volition. 'Is that why you married—because of the close family ties?'

He looked down at her and paused in his walk. They were near the main landing now, and the sounds of the house came clearly from below. A distant radio, voices from the hall, a sewing machine whirring.

'I married my wife because I loved her,' he said quietly.

'I'm sorry, I shouldn't have asked.' She felt choked, a lump in her throat, tears not far away.

'Of course you had the right. You are, in a sense, part of it now.'

'No, I'm not.' She shook her head. 'Only because of my resemblance—I was just curious, with her being American——'

'My uncle emigrated there years ago, from my father's home town in Greece.'

'You are Greek?'

'My father is, my mother was Russian. I was born in Lithuania.'

'Good grief!' Her lip trembled, partly laughter, partly tears, and he smiled.

'A mixture, am I not?'

'Somewhat. How fascinating. You must have relatives all over the place.'

'I do. Cousins and second cousins mainly. There is always someone to visit when I go abroad.' They were walking down the stairs now. 'And you, Polly, how about you? Do you have many relatives?'

'No. My mother died when I was sixteen—my father two years after, as you know. I have no one. Zoe and her husband have been very good friends to me, but ——' she shrugged.

'I'm sorry.'

'I'm used to it.' She gave him a bright smile.

'You must have many friends.' He opened the door to his study. 'Come in here, it is quiet, and you can sit for a while and talk.'

'I keep in touch with some old school chums——'

'And a boy-friend?' he replied.

She looked at him. 'No one special.' That was true. She had had several dates with a young reporter from the paper, but, while she enjoyed his company, she had no romantic feelings towards him. Polly attracted men, enjoyed flirting and dining out, but not one had ever caught her heart, and at twenty-five she sometimes wondered if she would ever meet the mythical 'Mr Right', the one man for her. She had a vague image of him at the back of her mind, of a strong, gentle man, a man who would love and be loved, someone with whom she could laugh, and cry, and relax totally. And sometimes the mental image of just such a man came to her, and—at that moment Boris Leander said something, and she met his eyes, and saw him blend with her mental image. She saw the strength and tenderness in his face, the hard eyes momentarily softened, that wide mouth curved in a smile—and she caught her breath at the shock of it.

'I'm sorry, what did you say?' She blinked, and everything was normal again.

'I said would you like a drink? It will soon be dinner time. Perhaps a sherry?'

'That would be nice.' She had had foolish imaginings because the afternoon visit had drained her. In a few weeks, surely no more, they would go out of each other's lives. She would be returned home to Wallington and take up her job on the paper, and perhaps she would look for his name from time to time, and wonder what he was doing.... Then she remembered. 'You had a reason for going to Wallington, didn't you?' she asked. 'I mean a reason apart from seeing your grandmother's home—ah, was that true?'

'Was what true? That I had an English grandmother? Yes. She married a Greek, my father's father. And what makes you say I had another reason? Something you heard?' he seemed amused as he handed her a glass.

'There's always talk in a place like that,' she evaded.

'How true! There is everywhere. Yes, I had another reason—but it is private at the moment.'

She felt herself pink. 'I'm not trying to pry,' she said quickly. It was better she didn't know anyway. She had promised herself that she would forget her job while she was there. It was the only way.

'But I will tell you anyway. I trust you, Polly.' She was to remember those words, later that night.

'I'd rather you didn't.' She sipped her sherry. 'I live there, remember? Please—don't.'

'It is not bad. In fact, just the opposite. However,' he shrugged, 'as you wish, of course.' She was to remember that, too. In fact she was to remember everything that had ever been said between them later that dreadful night. There was nothing to warn her, everything was calm, and she gradually felt herself relaxing in the peaceful atmosphere of his study, as she watched him light a cigar, go to the french windows, and open them to let in a cool evening breeze. He stood there, silhouetted with the light shining in on him, a dark outline partially blocking out the light, and she wondered how many women had loved him. And yet he, apparently, had loved only one—a woman who had looked so like she herself that she was able to act as her.

She told him then of what she had talked about to his father, and he turned, and listened to her attentively, nodding occasionally, face interested.

'Good,' he said. 'You were perfect. And you say there was some response?'

'I sensed he heard me, yes,' she answered. 'In fact I was worried in case my voice was too different from Crystal's—but I was speaking very quietly anyway, really a whisper.'

'Your voice is very similar, as a matter of fact. I meant to tell you that. In fact the total likeness is remarkable.'

'Doesn't it—hurt you?' she said softly. She didn't know why she had said it. He walked away from the window towards her. For one absurd moment she thought he was angry at her question.

'No.' He put his glass down carefully on the table. 'When I first saw you, at that meeting in the hotel——' she remembered that moment only too well, 'That was a—shock to me. It was like—seeing her again,' he spoke hesitantly, as if searching for the right words. 'It was like someone you had thought dead coming back to life.' He looked at her, his eyes shadowed and serious. 'But even as I looked at you, the idea came to me so strongly that it wiped all other considerations out of my mind. I knew I had to speak to you, to ask you. And once I make up my mind on something, I do it. Did I startle you?' He sat down as he spoke.

'Oh, yes, you did.' That was very true. She couldn't tell him that she had been about to speak to *him*, had actually been rehearsing the words in her mind when he had come over to her. Perhaps she should have done, then. But the moment passed. He went on:

'It was like fate, you being there as a guest. I knew if I didn't speak then, you might be gone.' She looked down at her glass. If only he knew the truth. That she had seen his wife's photograph, had gone there deliberately because of it....

'Well, you did—and here I am,' she said lightly. 'And

I shall go up and see your father again after dinner, because I promised I would. Then I'll have that early night I need.'

'You know I don't expect you to stay up there all the time. You must not tire yourself too much on my behalf. If there is nothing to amuse you here, you have only to say the word and I can arrange an evening out for you anywhere you choose.'

'I'm not a person who needs entertaining,' she said. 'Don't think that. It's perfectly relaxing here. I'll probably go swimming tomorrow, and Janet has promised to make me a long dress. She's good company—and there are all those books in the library——'

'I feel it is not enough.'

'Why? You didn't force me to come here, I chose to. And I'm well content as long as I'm helping your father in some small way.'

He looked at her. 'You are an unusual woman, Polly. You know that?'

She laughed. 'Why am I? I'm *me*—perfectly ordinary——'

'Not ordinary. Never say that about yourself. You are kind, you are warm and gentle, and you care—I remember you saying that to me. And now I know what you care about.'

The atmosphere changed. It became charged with the subtle undercurrents that seemed to fill the room in a shimmering tension. He moved restlessly, as if powerfully aware of it, stood up and went over to the cupboard to return with the sherry decanter. She shook her head and put her hand over her glass. 'No more for me, thanks.' Her heart was beating faster, although she didn't know why. Yet she was disturbed by him, and it was as if he too were disturbed without knowing the reason. 'I must go——' she began.

'Wait,' he said. 'I want to show you something——' He went to a cupboard and opened it. Inside were rows of drawers, neatly labelled. A filing cabinet within a normal cupboard, cleverly concealed. He lifted out an envelope and brought it across to her. Sitting down, he opened it and took out several glossy photographs. 'This is what I plan for Wallington,' he said.

Polly took them from him to see a photographed model of a long low factory buildings surrounded by trees, another of bungalows, a park, a school. 'I don't understand,' she said. 'These are scale models, aren't they?'

'Yes—of what I plan. Wallington is dying on its feet—you must know that—this will bring jobs and new life to the town. It's an electronics factory, manufacturing parts for watches, calculators, radios, etcetera.'

She was silent. He spoke the truth, though how had he found out? It wasn't the sort of thing emblazoned in newspapers. 'Wallington dying on its feet. . . .'

'And the factory will blend in with the landscape. I'm not a countryside polluter. There will be no high chimneys belching black smoke. The place will be surrounded by trees, and with a park, tennis courts, swimming pool. It will attract workers from all over the country—and I will build accommodation for them.'

So now, in just a few moments of easy conversation, she had discovered what Ed had sent her to the meeting to find out. And she couldn't tell him; she couldn't tell anyone. 'I take it the plans are well advanced?' she asked.

'Yes. Two of my representatives are having talks with the council next week. I have already talked and been given the go-ahead, in Whitehall.'

'You're very decisive, aren't you?'

'There's no room for negative thinking in my world.'

'I can see that.' She smiled and handed him back the photographs. 'Thank you for letting me see them.' She suddenly had to change the subject, in case he decided to ask casually where she worked in Wallington. It seemed yet another deception, yet she had no choice. And another opportunity, to tell the truth, passed. 'Was your father in business like you?' she asked.

'He guided me when I was young, and then told me I was on my own, to sink or swim—it was up to me.' He smiled slightly. 'I swam.'

'So I see,' she remarked dryly. 'You used to be a racing driver, didn't you?'

'That as well. To escape the boredom of business. I found it intensely boring at first—I sometimes still do. Does that surprise you?'

'No, why should it? My father always used to say that you can only sit in one chair or drive one car at a time. Anything else must be superfluous—mind you, he was never wealthy. But he was happy.' Her voice faltered as she thought of him.

'And a wise man,' he said gently.

'Yes. I think—I'd better go. I'd like to wash my hair before dinner. Perhaps Janet will help me with this new style she's given me.'

'I don't think that necessary. Your hair suits its curls. Leave it as you like it, please.'

'But your father——' she began.

'I don't think he would notice. Women change their hair often—that is not important any more. The important thing is over and above that—and in that you have succeeded. He thinks you *are* Crystal.'

She stood up, too shaken to answer, and Boris moved nearer, and put his hand lightly on her arm. 'For which I thank you.' She looked up into his eyes, and a tightness came into her throat. He exuded a masculinity that was almost overpowering. She felt as if she could not move away. She wanted him to kiss her, she wanted it very much.

'I must——' she began, and he moved, ever so slightly, his hands a featherlight caress upon her arms, round her shoulders, so strong, yet so gentle, and she was as helpless as a kitten, revelling in his touch, wanting it to go on for ever, wanting.... His mouth came down on hers, and she closed her eyes, and released from the spell of stillness, put her hands up to his neck, sensuously revelling in the warmth and power of him, and the sheer animal excitement of him. Their bodies were close, closer, touching, and her whole body tingled with the strength. The kiss went on, and changed, and the world swirled away into nothingness, and they were alone in it, and nothing else was there save the two of them, and nothing else mattered; she was filled with fire, a warmth she had never known before; she was lost.

He groaned, he took hold of her, he carried her to the settee, then she was truly in his arms, and now she knew he was going to make love to her—and it was all she had ever wanted, and it would be wonderful, because she knew now what she should have known since she first saw him walk into that room at the Wallington Arms. This was the man she had dreamed of all her life. 'The door,' she whispered, easing his weight as she moved slightly to make them both more comfortable.

'No one ever comes in,' he murmured in her ear, and kissed it, then moved his lips in a path of fire along her cheek until he found her mouth, forced it open, kissed her so deeply she could scarcely breathe, and his hands were on her breast now, teasing and touching so gently that she wanted to cry out——

And perhaps she had, for the next moment the room was filled with the sound of the knocking at the door. She saw Boris's face, in that moment before he lifted himself away from her, and it was the face of such intense anger that she instinctively recoiled, as in a harsh voice he said: 'Who is that?'

'Me, Mr Leander. Miss Summers is wanted urgently on the telephone.'

'Just a minute.' He looked at her, two silent conspirators, pulled her to her feet in one easy movement, brushed her cheek with his lips, and whispered: 'If I kill her now, don't be surprised.'

'No.' Polly was too shaken to move away. She clung to him briefly, still trembling.

'You'd better go.' He pushed her gently away. It was unspoken, implicit. No words were needed. But it was there, lingering in the air: 'Afterwards——'

She opened the door to see Mrs Harris waiting. Polly looked at her, and now she could almost smile. 'I'll take it in my room,' she said, and closed the study door after her. She felt reckless, heady; she didn't care about what she saw in the housekeeper's eyes. She didn't care about anything at that moment. The reckless excitement still filled her, and the whole world was part of it.

She walked past Mrs Harris, and away, up the stairs, not looking back. It would most likely be Zoe. It would be interesting to see how long she had been hanging on, how long Lena Harris had been hovering outside the door before knocking—and what she had heard.

She went into her room and closed the door, went over to the window and picked up the telephone.

And that telephone call changed everything.

CHAPTER SIX

POLLY went to see Boris's father after dinner. The atmosphere at the meal had been unusual, to say the least. Mrs Harris had served them, with a maid, and she had been silent, efficient, not smiling. Boris had talked about casual matters, yet the atmosphere had had those exciting undercurrents that filled her so that she could scarcely eat. Their eyes had met briefly and often, and in them Polly had seen the warmth that coursed through her own veins, yet on the surface his manner was that of the perfect host.

I love him, she thought in wonder, I love him as I've never loved any man before, and he loves me, I'm sure of it. . . .

'Coffee in here, Mr Leander?' Mrs Harris's voice cut in on her warm dream, and she scarcely heard his reply. Then a telephone call had come for him, as Mrs Harris poured the coffee, an urgent call from America.

'Will you excuse me, Polly?' he had said.

'Of course. I'll drink this, then go up to your father.'

He took his cup out with him, and Mrs Harris carefully poured Polly's coffee out. 'Cheese and biscuits, Miss Summers?' she asked.

Polly looked at her. 'No, thanks.' What was in her face? A gleam of suppressed excitement, a glow she didn't understand. Her heart thudded in sudden fear. She didn't like that look.

'Very well. Will you excuse me now?'

'Certainly.' At the door, the housekeeper glanced back briefly at Polly. This time there could be no mistake. The hatred that flashed towards her was mingled with triumph. She closed the door softly and Polly was alone.

She began to feel uneasy. Finishing her coffee, she left the table and went out, and up the stairs. What on earth——

In the antiseptic, hospital-style room in which Boris's father lay, she soon forgot the uneasiness brought by the housekeeper's look. She sat there, allowing the nurse on duty her well-earned coffee break, took the old man's hand, and began the one-sided conversation she was now getting used to. It was getting easier on every visit to relax and be herself. In a strange way she felt she was getting to know the man who lay so still and unmoving. A warm bond was being established between them, and when, near the end of her visit, he moved his other hand, reached out to touch her arm, she felt such a glow of pride that she wanted to rush out and tell someone, preferably Boris. She squeezed his hand gently.

'I know you're getting better,' she said. 'Soon we'll be going out in the gardens for a walk.'

He seemed to be making the effort to speak. She sensed the time it took him, and whispered: 'It's all right. Take your time, gently now.'

'A walk,' the voice was a whisper, but unmistakable. 'We will walk—in the garden, Crystal. Soon.'

It was the most he had ever said. She was nearly crying with joy. 'Yes, my dear, very soon,' she said, heart bursting. She leaned over to kiss the waxen cheek, and a tear dropped from her eye. She smoothed it away with a finger, and he whispered:

'You weep, my child?'

'For joy, Poppa, because you are better. Rest now.'

'Is it evening?'

'Yes. Would you like me to come in and say good-night later?'

'Yes.'

'Then I shall. Rest now, Poppa.'

She went out quietly, saw the nurse, and took her arm. 'He's been talking to me,' she said, eyes shining.

'He's improving,' said the nurse, a blue-eyed Irish girl with a gentle face. 'Thank God—it's a miracle, no less. The doctor remarked on it today.' She grabbed hold of Polly's hands impulsively. 'Sure and I've not seen anything like it before. Bless you, Miss Summers.'

'I'll go and tell Mr Leander.' That was her first priority. To tell the man she loved that his father could speak. She ran out, light-footed, along the corridor, down the stairs, into the hall. Mrs Harris was emerging from the drawing room. 'Where's Mr Leander?' she asked her, unaware of the woman's expression.

'In his study——' she began. 'But he's busy——' her face twisted into a smile. It was not a pleasant smile. 'Very busy——'

'This is important.' Polly was in a state of euphoria, and nothing mattered. How could he mind being interrupted by such news as she had?

She tapped on his door, and his voice called: 'Come in.' She went in, bursting with the news, and as she did so, he put down the telephone.

'Boris, he's better—he spoke to me——' she faltered into silence at the expression on his face, and took an instinctive step nearer to him. 'Boris, what——'

'Don't come any nearer,' he said harshly. 'I might not be responsible for my actions.' And she saw a deep dark anger in his face, like nothing she had ever seen before on anyone. He was toweringly, thunderously angry—and the anger, coming across the room in waves, was directed solely at her.

Polly stood transfixed, face white with shock. 'What—is it?' she whispered. 'What——'

'You did your work well, didn't you?' his voice lashed her. 'Have you been sending daily reports home? Or are you saving them until you can take photographs to cover the story better?'

She sank on to the settee, her legs too weak to support her from the dreadful force of his words and he stepped across and yanked her to her feet, his fingers biting into her arms. 'Don't sit down,' he grated, 'you will stand while I talk to you.'

He was hurting her physically, but his anger was even more painful. It was stupefying agony, and she couldn't escape it, or move. And even then she didn't realise. . . .

'Do you know who I have just been phoning? I will

tell you. My contacts in Wallington. I have been check-
ing up on you, because I was not prepared to believe
what Mrs Harris told me——' Then she knew. She
knew everything. She knew that the click on the telephone line had not been imagined. And she remembered what Zoe had been talking about, before that
quiet, triumphant click had come—and she wanted to
die.

'Oh, no——' she whispered. 'Boris, believe me, it's
not——'

'It is. And you are. You are a reporter on the *Wallington Courier*, and the man with whom you stay is Ed
Welsh, the editor——'

'Yes, but——'

He flung her from him so violently that she fell,
sprawling, against the settee, putting her hands up instinctively to shield her body from blows. 'No,' he
said, 'I would not strike you—I would not *touch* you
—if I did, I might kill you.' He looked angry enough to
do it. White-faced, taut, a muscle moving in his cheek,
his eyes blazing, he stood there, and he *towered* over
her, a veritable giant of a man. Yet strangely enough,
in the midst of his anger, she began to regain her own
strength. No one had ever treated her or spoken to her
like that ever before. So it was all over. He knew who
she was, he hated reporters, and he had a temper on
him the like of which she had never seen before—and
no one ever answered him back, or dared to cross him.
She could understand that. She could see exactly why.
But suddenly she no longer cared. She jumped to her

feet and faced him, eyes blazing, and, putting her hands on her hips, took a deep breath.

'Listen, *you*!' she said. 'Just listen to me. Yes, I am a reporter on the *Courier*. I've been working on it for a month or so—and Ed took me to that meeting in the hopes I'd get a chance to interview you as to your reasons for coming to Wallington. He showed me a photograph—but I didn't want to go, yet I went, because he's been like a father to me——'

'Shut up!' he blazed. 'You little tramp——'

He got no further. Polly hit him with all her strength across his lean hard face. There was an instant's electric, explosive silence, then she burst out: 'Don't you *dare* call me a tramp!'

'Was it part of your job? To get me to bed? Is it *that* kind of paper——'

She launched herself on him, incensed, too angry herself now to retain a vestige of self-control, pummelled his chest and shoulders, sobbing, reaching for his face, and was caught in a grip of steel, twisted round so that she was facing away from him, and held powerless.

'You little hellcat,' he grated. 'My God, I'd like to beat you!'

'You wouldn't dare—let me go!' she struggled wildly.

'I dare anything I choose. Unfortunately I don't fight women.'

She kicked his leg violently and was rewarded by being twisted round to face him. Sobbing, panting, she stared up into his face, the tears coursing down her cheeks. 'I came here because you *asked* me to,' she sobbed. 'I came to *help*. I swear I told no one—only Zoe—why I was here. Ed doesn't know——'

'You lie! You said it was he who took you——'

'Only to *interview* you, that's all. Do you think *I* knew about your father? Did anyone?' A pulse beat in her throat. She thought she was going to faint. 'Phone Zoe. Ask her. You're—h-hurting me——' The room began to swim round, going darker, and she moaned softly. 'Ask——' She felt herself going heavy, and there was a rushing, roaring sound in her ears and head, then everything went a merciful blankness.

She opened her eyes, and she was on the settee. Boris Leander stood watching her a few feet away. The terrible anger had abated slightly, yet still he was like a man in the grip of intense emotion, his face white, eyes darkened with the vestiges of his temper. Polly rubbed her arms where he had held her. She was breathing raggedly, and felt exhausted.

'Phone her,' she whispered. 'If you won't—I'll leave tonight——'

'Leave? Now? And kill my father?'

She looked up, bewildered. 'But you d-don't——' she stammered, 'don't want me to s-stay——'

'There is no choice.' He almost spat the words out. 'I am not prepared to let you go at this stage. Regardless of who you are, what you are——'

She lifted her chin. 'I'm still useful? Is that it? Thanks for nothing! Aren't you scared I might be sending out those daily reports to my contacts on Fleet Street?' her lips quivered. 'Why don't you search my room?' she added in contempt.

'Mrs Harris already has. She found nothing.'

She jumped to her feet. 'How dare she! How dare you! *That* woman——'

'I can trust her.'

'Oh, I'm sure you can. But then she's in love with you—or hadn't you noticed?'

'Don't be stupid.'

'Don't be stupid,' she mimicked. 'It's you that's stupid. You haven't seen the way she looks at me. My God, she hates me! I don't suppose you *thought* to ask her why she eavesdropped on my call, did you? Or do you make a habit of it with all your guests?'

'It was by mere accident. She waited until you picked up your bedroom extension before putting her own phone down—only she happened to overhear Zoe's first words——'

'Happened to overhear! Ha! And did she also tell you how long she'd "happened" to be listening outside this door while you were trying to make love to me? I'll tell *you*. Zoe had been holding on for six minutes! She was about to give up when I got on the line.' She did something very swiftly and suddenly. She turned, flung open the study door, and called to the swiftly retreating housekeeper: 'Don't go away, Mrs Harris, you were just going to hear something interesting about yourself.' She turned to Boris. 'There you are.'

He had followed her to the door. The housekeeper's

face was contorted with a terrible anger. That makes two of you, thought Polly. She was beginning to feel drained of all strength.

Boris spoke quietly. 'I'll speak to you afterwards, Lena.' The woman looked at him, then with venom at Polly.

'There's nothing to say, Mr Leander,' she spat out. 'She's said it all. Are you going to believe her lies——'

'That's enough!' His voice was an icy whiplash.

'Oh, no, it isn't!' she snapped. Her face was white, almost grey. 'I've had enough of this farce. Send her away—she's trouble——'

He opened the door. 'You'd better come in. I don't intend having a scene in the hall.'

Mrs Harris seemed to hover, indecisive, then, taking a deep breath, she marched into his study. Boris closed the door and faced her, and Polly backed away. This was, in a way, nothing to do with her at the moment. This was another fight. Yet she trembled inwardly.

'This farce, Mrs Harris?' he said. 'What do you mean?'

'Her—pretending to be your——' her voice faltered at the expression on his face, 'your late wife—it's obscene——'

'That is nothing to do with you. Your job here is as housekeeper—do you understand? Taking care of the smooth running of my house. *That* is what you are paid for, not to comment on my decisions. You don't run my life, Mrs Harris, and never have, never will. I hope I make myself clear. I will not have you listening at doors——'

'If I hadn't listened in on a phone call you wouldn't have found out what *she* was up to,' she said. 'Don't you *see*, I did it for you——'

'So you did. And now I know, and am dealing with the situation in my own way. That doesn't give you licence to go eavesdropping all over the place——'

'Do you believe her?' she shrilled.

'It seems rather odd to me that you should be walking away from the door at the moment Miss Summers opened it. You are normally in the kitchen at this time.'

'She's poisoning you against me!' The woman whirled on Polly, who had stood silently listening to the exchange with a growing horror. 'You lying little bitch——'

'Silence!' his voice cut in harshly.

'I won't be silent,' she shrieked. '*You* called her a liar and a little tramp——' she stopped, and in the mounting silence it was clear that she knew she had just given herself away.

'So you *were* listening,' he said softly. 'Do you think I can ever trust you again, now?'

'I'm not leaving!' she gasped. 'You can't——'

'I can. You will leave in the morning. I shall give you three month's salary in lieu of notice. I suggest you pack your things tonight——'

'Oh, *God*,' the woman covered her face and began to wail. 'Please—no, Mr Leander—Boris! No, don't, I beg you—you don't know what it means to be here, near you——' Polly turned away feeling faintly sick. She wanted to walk out, to escape, but there was no escape.

'Pull yourself together, woman. You've been valuable to me, but to do what you did and expect me to still——'

Mrs Harris raised a ravaged face to him. 'No,' she said. 'No—you mustn't send me away. I know too much.' The last words fell into the air like stones dropping into water. There was a dreadful clarity and finality to them. Boris Leander seemed to grow, to become more solid—and deadly.

'What do you mean?' he said, each word spaced evenly.

She shook her head. 'Can't you *guess*?' Her eyes were wild. 'Don't you think everyone wants to know about *you*?' Why do you think *she's* here? The papers will queue up to buy——'

'To buy the private details of my life for publication? I see—you're trying a little blackmail, are you?' His voice went very, very cold. 'I don't like blackmail. I don't even like the word. It is ugly. You are ugly. Get out of my sight!'

'You'll regret it.' She stood her ground. She was like a woman fighting for her life. Polly knew if she stayed in the room a moment longer she would be ill. She went quickly to the door, hand over mouth, and ran out. The words from Boris that followed her as she went were etched in her brain.

'Will I? Then perhaps it is time for me to be equally frank——' she heard no more. She was concentrating on getting to her room before she was ill.

*

Polly lay on her bed. An hour had passed since the dreadful scene in the study, and she wondered if she would ever have the strength to move again. She had heard no more sounds. Nothing. The house might have been totally empty.

She had promised to visit the invalid again, and would keep that promise. And before she went, she had to clear her mind of all the blurred emotion that filled it. She had to be calm; that was most important. Calm and cool. She had to forget what she had seen on Boris Leander's face.

His father was a dying man, everyone knew that, knew that in a week, or two weeks, he would die. Polly talked as she did, of walks in the garden, of when he would be better, because that was the only way to talk to one so ill. Yet she knew in her heart it would not be. Soon she would be released from her task, and she knew now that she would feel the pain of his going as acutely as if she were really his daughter-in-law.

She went to wash her face, to apply more lipstick and comb the rebellious curls. She looked in the mirror to see her white, drawn face staring back at her. She pinched her cheeks to add colour, applied the perfume to wrists and neck, and she was ready. In the time it took her to walk to the other wing of the house she composed herself, and when she tapped on the outer door of the apartment she was to all intents and purposes normal.

The Irish nurse was sitting knitting, and stood up

when Polly went in. 'Mr Leander is with his father,' she said, smiling. 'Please go in.'

'Oh!' Polly was momentarily flustered. 'I'll wait——'

'No, go on. He expects you.'

He does? she thought. Oh, no, not again—it was a brief thought, quickly dismissed. At least she would be safe from his anger in there. Probably the only place in the house that that could be guaranteed. She wondered if Mrs Harris had left.... 'Right. Wish me luck.'

The little nurse crossed her fingers. 'I think you bring your own luck with you,' she smiled. 'He's so much better each time *you* visit.'

Polly tiptoed into the second room, and Boris was sitting on a chair by his father's bed, talking quietly to him. He looked up as Polly entered, said: 'Here she is, Father,' and stood up, motioning Polly to his chair.

'Hello, Poppa, I'm back—as promised.' She bent over to kiss him, then sat down in the chair. Boris drew up another one, sat at the other side of the bed, and watched her. She could have been unnerved, but she wasn't. Here, in this room, there would never be any unpleasantness. It was as if a truce existed. She began to talk, softly, soothingly, and gradually she found herself becoming truly calm. It was not a one-sided conversation. Boris took part, and the old man said a few words from time to time. Not without effort—but Polly could see the effect they had on his son. It was as if something startling and new was happening. She remembered that she had not been given a chance to tell him, before. . . .

The nurse tapped on the door, and came in. 'Dr Roberts is here, Mr Leander,' she said. 'He was passing——' a glance was exchanged, and Boris stood up.

'Then we'll let him come in. Come, Crystal dear, we'll return in a few minutes, Father.'

The doctor, a tall spare man, balding, was waiting in the outer room. He and Boris shook hands. 'The nurse told me of the improvement when I telephoned this evening,' he said. 'I thought I would call and see for myself. You will wait, sir?'

'Of course.' The doctor and nurse vanished, the door closed. Polly went over to the window and looked out. There was no need for pretence here. This was not the magic place.

'He is better,' he said.

She didn't turn round. 'Yes, I know.' She concentrated on watching a pair of doves pecking at the lawn outside. Then suddenly she sensed he had moved nearer, and her skin prickled. He made no sound; she sensed his nearness, as though he had touched her, but he hadn't. Near was too near.

'Has Mrs Harris gone?' she asked.

'Yes.'

'I know *my* place now,' she said. 'I will not trespass. I will not speak unless spoken to—except here. Here is different.' She turned to face him. 'I will spend most of my time here. And the only things I shall talk about to your father will be trivial and light—the kind of things he needs to hear.' The bitterness she could not hide was in her voice, and it came spilling out. 'And please take the telephone out of my room. If I phone, or receive a call, I will take it somewhere where you can listen.' She turned away again.

A brittle, electric tension filled the room, almost stifling. And he moved away without answering her. She wondered if it was because he didn't know what to say. But something told her it was not that; that she would pay for her reckless words. She gripped the windowsill—then the inner door opened, and the doctor came out.

'A word with you both, please,' he said. 'Nurse Ryan is giving him a wash—Mr Leander, I can only describe the change in your father's condition as something quite beyond my experience. I would like a second opinion. May I bring a colleague tomorrow?'

'Certainly. Dr Roberts, are you saying that there is hope for my father?'

The doctor smiled. 'I'm not putting it as definitely as that, sir,' he answered. 'But let me put it this way. I would have expected a gradual deterioration in his condition at this time, after that massive stroke—but it has been arrested. Not only that, but he has definitely regained the power of speech to a remarkable extent. And until Dr Johnson has been with me, I'd rather not say more.' He looked across at Polly, who was standing very still, listening.

'The improvement dates from your arrival, madam.'

He nodded to her. 'The nursing profession needs people like you.' He smiled warmly at her. 'I'll go now. Nurse Ryan will be out in a moment or two, then you can go in.'

'Doctor, is there any time limit to our visits?'

'Normally I would say yes, but having seen him, I would say no. Stay as long as you like—don't tire your-selves, of course. I appreciate it can be wearing, talking to an invalid like that, but he thrives—is thriving—on these visits. The more time you can spend—the better. Good evening to you both.' He nodded briskly and went out. They were alone again. The relief from tension was too great for Polly. She put her hands to her face, and a sob was wrenched from her. She went to the nurse's chair and sat down blindly, not seeing anything.

'Polly——' she heard his voice.

'No. Please—don't say anything.' Her voice was muffled. 'Please—I couldn't bear it. Don't worry. I'll be all right to go in when the nurse comes out.' She fumbled for a handkerchief in her bag and wiped her eyes. The sobs subsided, she became more calm. Diffi-cult with him there, but she did it because she had to. And when, a minute or so afterwards, Nurse Ryan came out, she was quite composed.

The second visit was longer, and now it was as if a rapport was building up between the three of them. There was even laughter, over something Boris said, about a visit to 'The Castle', then the old man began to chuckle, and Polly joined in, as if she knew what it was about, even though she didn't. Then Boris's father said, haltingly, to her:

'We will walk in together, eh, my dear—that will surprise them all.'

'Indeed it will.' She hoped desperately that he wouldn't ask her any questions she couldn't answer about the Castle—whatever, wherever it was, and looked briefly to Boris, her face questioning.

'And where will I be?' he said smoothly. 'Waiting outside? A fine thing that, to see my wife going into the castle where we married with another man on her arm.'

Light dawned. And where else would they have wed? Nothing so normal as a church. 'We'll let you join us,' she said to Boris. 'Won't we, Poppa?'

He squeezed her hand. 'On your anniversary, we'll go. I'll surprise everybody.'

'You've already amazed Dr Roberts,' said Boris. 'He's bringing a colleague to see you tomorrow. I think he's very pleased with himself.'

'As well he might be,' said Polly lightly.

'Thanks—to you——' whispered the old man. He was tiring now, that could be seen clearly.

'I'll have to go now,' said Polly. 'Janet's going to make me a dress—for our evening out, Poppa. Sleep well. I'll see you in the morning.' She bent over him to kiss him, and went out. She said goodnight to the nurse, and fled. She didn't want to walk anywhere with Boris. To-morrow she would ask Janet if she could have breakfast in her room. If she managed to avoid him altogether, it would be sensible. There was no reason why it couldn't be done. If she had her way, the only times they met would be with his father. He had hurt her far more deeply than she cared to admit, even to herself. He would not get the chance again.

She went into her bedroom and pressed the bell on the wall at the side of her bed. Then she switched on the television, leaving the sound very quiet, and went into her bathroom to wash.

There came a knock on the bedroom door as she was drying her face, and she called out: 'Come in, Janet. Sit down, I'll not be a moment.'

She heard the door open, then close. A quick flick with her comb, and she was ready. 'Janet,' she began, 'you remember you offered to——' she walked into the bedroom.

But it wasn't Janet who stood there. It was Boris.

CHAPTER SEVEN

POLLY'S words faded with the shock. She looked at him, and she couldn't speak. She drew a deep breath. 'I rang for Janet,' she said, 'and I'm expecting her——'

'I know. I told her I wanted to speak to you first,' he said.

'But there is nothing to say. Don't you think you said it all before?' she returned.

'Not quite.'

'Mr Leander——' she used the words deliberately. 'I'm very tired, after all that's happened. I know this is your house, but you gave me this bedroom while I am here—is it too much to ask you to leave a room in *your* house?' She stood firm and faced him. 'It is the only place where I thought I could be sure of being alone, if I wished.' She pointed to the telephone. 'If you've come to remove that, please do so. It shouldn't be too much trouble—it is the plug-in type, isn't it?'

'I haven't come for that.' His voice was harsh. 'I came to talk about my father with you.' He looked round. 'I shall, of course, respect your privacy——'

'Thank you,' she cut in, with irony.

He ignored her words. 'But I must talk with you, in view of the fact that he is now speaking and may start referring to things you know nothing about—and expect you to know the answers.'

It was eminently logical. Polly had thought about it while they had been in his father's room. 'However,' he went on, 'if you prefer not to talk here—then may we do so downstairs?'

'I suppose so. Where?'

'In my study.'

'I'll be down in a few minutes.' She waited for him to go. He looked at her silently for a moment, then turned and went out, closing the door quietly behind him. She let out her breath in a huge sigh and went to sit on the bed. 'Phew!' she said slowly. She leaned on one of the posts of the bed, and fanned her face with her hand. She had gone unaccountably warm. There was hostility in every line of him, and she felt uncomfortable. My God, she thought, I don't know how much more I can take. She prayed that the interview in his study would be brief, picked up her bag, and went slowly down the stairs.

He was waiting for her by the window in his study, looking out at a darkening sky as she went in. He turned, taking his time. 'Would you like a drink?'

'No, thank you.'

'Please sit down.' He indicated a chair.

'I'd rather stand, if you don't mind.'

'Very well.' He walked across towards her, stopped a few feet away, and added: 'I'll try and be brief.'

'Please do.'

'You're making this very difficult for me.'

'I'm not trying to make it easy,' she shot back. 'Do you expect me to?'

She didn't give a damn about him any more. To think she had imagined herself to be in love with him! She went cold with horror at the idea. She saw his face change, and with it, the crackling undercurrents of tension, sparking around them, filling the room. He was holding himself in check and she sensed he wasn't used to it. He certainly would not be used to anyone answering him as she was doing.

'No,' he answered. 'I don't. But you might as well listen to what I have to say because it is important.'

'I know that. It concerns your father—that's why I'll listen. On any other subject I'd rather we both keep to our own opinions.' Her eyes were cold and angry, and she made no attempt to hide her contempt. He had said things she would never forget—unforgivable things. 'I'll even make notes if you think there's a lot I need to know.'

'As you wish. Hadn't you better sit down at my desk to do so?'

'Yes.' She marched across, put her bag down and walked round to the chair behind the desk.

Boris opened a drawer, took out several sheets of plain paper and a pen, and set them down in front of her. 'Ready?' he asked.

'Yes.'

'The castle my father referred to is near here— Durden Castle. We were married there six years ago on September the twentieth.' He paused to allow her to write. 'There is a chapel attached to the castle, and the ceremony was performed by the Reverend Arthur Staines, at twelve noon. The reception afterwards was in the banqueting hall—which my father was referring to. Every so often they give medieval banquets—the three of us went to one shortly after the wedding. He may refer to it, so I will give you details of that in case he wants to talk about it.'

Her pen flew across the paper, and she could almost see the place as he described it, his voice soft, reminiscent. . . .

Half an hour later she had filled three sheets of

paper with details of the time he and Crystal had shared, and it was like an intrusion into someone else's private, innermost life. She felt exhausted. She had been tired before, but this was more drastic than that. When he had finished, she looked up, white-faced. 'Is that all?' she asked.

'Yes.'

She looked down at the papers, and they blurred and danced. 'Thank God!' she whispered.

'You need a drink.'

'No, I'm going. We've talked. Have you said all you wanted to say?' She stood up, and she swayed slightly with dizziness. Hastily she steadied herself on the desk.

'Yes. Are you all right, Polly?'

She looked up. 'No, I'm not. But then you'd hardly expect me to be after your attack on me before, would you? Don't worry, I'll be fine in the morning—as long as you leave me alone——' She had to sit down again before the room started spinning too violently. The next moment he was round the desk, by her side, his hands on her shoulders.

'Polly——' he said. His voice seemed to come from far away. She noted, even in the midst of the turmoil, that the touch of his hands was gentle. Not a bit like it had been before. It was too much effort; she could scarcely think, let alone move to escape. As he helped her up she made no resistance, allowed him to lead her to the settee, at the back of her mind the confused thought of what had so nearly happened there before. Then she was down, lying back, feet up, shoes off, and he vanished, to return with a glass of amber liquid.

'Brandy,' he said. 'Sip it.'

'I don't want——'

'Drink.' She drank. The room began to settle down, and she swallowed some more, then handed him the glass.

'That was stupid of me,' she said, 'but I'm all right now.' She stood up. 'I'm going to bed. Tell Janet I'll see her tomorrow.' A thought struck her. 'Does she know—what happened?'

'Yes. It is hardly anything that could be kept secret. Mrs Harris made sure of that.'

Would Janet now be hostile, knowing that she was from a newspaper? Polly closed her eyes briefly. 'Oh, is she still to——' it was difficult to phrase what she wanted to say—'help me?'

'Of course.' He knew what she meant.

'Then I'll go. Goodnight.' She clutched the papers and went to the door. Boris opened it for her. 'Thank you.'

'Goodnight,' he said. Polly went out. She would be safe in her own room. A haven of peace, away from him. So many things had happened she could scarcely think straight. She fell into bed fifteen minutes later, and was asleep as soon as her head touched the pillow.

Janet brought her breakfast up the following morning, and as she came in the room Polly scanned her face for any signs of hostility. She didn't think she could bear it if there were. She had come to like Janet in the brief time she had been at Leander House. There were none. Janet gave her a warm smile and said: 'Guess what? I've been promoted to housekeeper until Mr Leander gets someone else.'

Guiltily aware that if it hadn't been for her Mrs Harris would still be there, Polly answered: 'Is that what you want?'

'It makes a change!' Janet handed her the tray. 'I'm sorry about all the unpleasantness. I'd be a hypocrite if I said I'm sorry she's gone, because I'm not. But as for you being a reporter——' she shrugged, 'that's rotten luck—for you, I mean. He really hates them.'

'He hates me,' Polly whispered.

'No, he doesn't, you do so much for old Mr Leander——'

'I should have told him when he first asked me to come, then it would have been up to him. I made the terrible mistake of keeping quiet. He wiped the floor with me when that woman told him.'

'And you don't know why, do you?' Janet asked softly.

'Why what?' Polly gave her a puzzled look.

'Why he hates reporters?'

'No. Does he have to have a reason? He's a law unto himself——'

'Yes, true. No one else knows this, only Tom and I, and it was Tom who found out by accident—and I'm going to tell you, because I like you and I know I can trust you—when she—his wife was killed, she wasn't just on an ordinary plane trip. She was leaving him.'

'Oh, my God!' Polly, shattered, nearly dropped her coffee cup.

'There's worse, love.' Janet's face showed her own anguish. 'She was with another man—her lover. He was a top Fleet Street journalist who had been doing a series of articles about Boris—Mr Leander I mean, about all his various businesses. Mr Leander had trusted him, only——' she faltered.

'Janet, don't say any more. It's better I don't——'

'It's nearly over.' She was wringing her hands, the knuckles white. 'All the time, he'd been seeing Crystal —and one day they just left. There was a letter—I saw his face after he'd read it, just before the news came through. I never want to see anything like that again.' She looked towards the window, tears glinting in her eyes. 'That's it. The articles were never printed, of course. And everything else was hushed up. But now you know, at least, why he can't bear anything to do with newspapers——'

'I'm glad you've told me,' whispered Polly. 'And you knew—Crystal—you said how like her I was when I came—how could she do such a thing? They'd only been married a year—how can——'

'Polly, she was a bitch.' The words dropped into the still air, and Polly froze.

'Janet——'

'I know, you shouldn't speak ill of the dead. Then God forgive me, but she was. She was selfish—really selfish, I mean, the sort that have to have their own way in everything, all the time, regardless of who's hurt. Oh, she was charming as well. She was witty, and very beautiful, and old Mr Leander doted on her —she could twist him round her little finger. The trouble was, she couldn't do the same with her own husband—and it showed.'

'But he loved her,' said Polly gently.

'Yes, he did. But I sometimes wonder——' she paused and looked at Polly.

'Yes? You wonder?'

'If he still did when she was killed.'

'But he's never looked at another woman——'

'No, true. He's very bitter——'

'Oh, God!'

'I shouldn't have said so much. But I had to, knowing what happened. I couldn't keep silent knowing what you'd be going through——'

'I shan't say a word. I just feel awful about the whole thing.'

'I know—don't. Just remember one thing, the most important thing of all: what you're doing for old Mr Leander. The nurses have their meals with us, and they're full of what you do. Don't forget that, Polly.'

'I know. I'm very fond of him. It's tiring sometimes, but I'd stay there all day if I could. I can sense a difference in him already.'

'There is a big change. Keep that in mind when *he* gets you down.' She stood up. 'I'll let you have your breakfast. Just let me know whenever you want me.'

'I will. Thanks.' Polly watched her leave. She had had an insight into Boris's behaviour, and in a way it made her feel better about his undoubted dislike of her. She would manage somehow, come what may. There were further surprises in store for her, but as she ate her breakfast she was mercifully unaware of them.

She went along half an hour later to visit Poppa, as she was now coming to think of him. He was alone, with just the nurse, who looked up as Polly went in and stood up.

'Morning, Mrs Leander,' she greeted Polly. 'The doctor will be here soon—shall I have time for a coffee while you're here?'

'Of course,' Polly smiled. 'Off you go. I'll ring if the doctors arrive.'

She kissed the old man and sat beside the bed. There was, suddenly, an even warmer bond between them, in the light of what she now knew. 'You're looking better every day,' she whispered. 'I think you're pretending to be ill, just so you can have a fuss.' He chuckled. It was little more than a croak, but his eyes regarded her with more life than they had ever had before.

'You—tease—me,' he managed.

'Of course I'm teasing you, Poppa,' she laughed. 'I like seeing you laugh.'

'Where's my son?' he said.

'He'll be along soon, love. Very soon.'

The old man's hand tightened on hers, and he suddenly said: 'Where—your ring?'

'My—ring?' He had hold of her left hand. She normally sat on the other side of his bed.

'Wedding ring?'

'Oh, *that*!' she laughed, mind desperately searching. 'I lost weight—Boris sent it to be made a fraction smaller——' Did Crystal wear an engagement ring as well? She could hardly ask.

'Ah. But you're still as beautiful as ever. I knew one day you'd return——' It was the most he had ever said. It was also the most potentially dangerous situation, without Boris there. Any minute now, he might ask her a question. One she could not answer.

Thinking fast, Polly said: 'You know, Poppa, now you're so much better, how would it be if I read to you some time? I could stay much longer, and give that nice nurse an hour or so off. Would you like that?'

'Would you, my dear?'

'Of course. There are so many books here——'

'And you remember my favourites?' Out of the frying pan, she thought, what now?

'Well——' she said cautiously, 'let me think——' she frowned. 'I've a terrible memory just lately——'

'Conan Doyle,' he prompted slyly.

'Sherlock Holmes?' gently enquiring.

'Ah, yes, you remembered! But you must be busy——'

'I'll do *anything* for you, anything,' she whispered. And at that moment Boris walked in. She looked up at him, all calm again, all knowledge put firmly to the back of her mind. 'Remind me to look out a few Sherlock Holmes books, darling,' she said. It was a wonder she didn't choke over that last word, but she didn't. 'I'm going to read to Poppa.'

'Good.' He leaned over to kiss his father. 'You must be getting better.'

'I've told Poppa about the ring. He wondered where it was.' She looked at him over his father's head. 'I would have lost it if you hadn't suggested having it made smaller. It'll be ready soon, won't it?'

'Should be today or tomorrow. I'll phone them after.' He smiled easily at them both. She hoped he knew what he was saying. Today? One thing was sure—Mr Leander would expect her to be wearing a ring, if not today, certainly tomorrow. Her mind refused to think further on the subject.

Boris took over the conversation. The doctor had telephoned, he told his father, and would be there shortly. And he was taking Crystal out for a little ride, but they would visit when they returned, and was there anything he would like from the shops in Edinburgh?

'Edinburgh Rock,' the old man said, after some thought. 'You know how I like that.'

'It's a promise,' Boris laughed. He began talking about some business deal involving a friend of his father's, a perfectly innocuous story, and Polly could relax and let her mind flow over what Janet had told her, things that had, in a way, put a whole new complexion on the situation. She watched Boris as he spoke to his father, saw the hard lines of his face soften as he talked, sensed the depth there was to him, the pain he must have been through, and her heart filled with an awareness of him, and she ached for him. She moved uneasily in her chair, and Boris looked across at her.

'All right, darling?' he asked. She would have sworn, if she hadn't known otherwise, that the concern in his voice was genuine.

'Of course.' She laughed. 'I was just listening.'

'But—forgive me—it must be boring for you to listen to talk of finance.'

'Of course not. To be honest though, I was just thinking what I might buy in Edinburgh.'

'You may buy anything you choose.'

Mr Leander spoke. 'Crystal, buy a pretty dress for me—I will pay. Will you do that?'

She was about to refuse, and saw Boris's warning nod. 'How kind of you, Poppa. I'd love to. I shall wear it for you tonight.'

The old man smiled, contented, and there came a knock at the door and in walked the nurse. 'Dr Roberts is here, sir,' she said, 'with Dr Johnson.'

'Send them in, nurse,' said Boris, standing up. 'Crystal, go and get yourself ready for your ride. I will stay here a few minutes, and see you downstairs.'

'Of course. 'Bye, Poppa. See you later. I won't forget the rock!'

She went out, bidding the two waiting doctors good morning, and fled to her room. There she stood just inside the door, hand to mouth, the memory of a brief pain she had seen in Boris's eyes when they had been in his father's room, and she had mentioned the wedding ring. Gone in an instant, yet it had been there.

Had it brought back a bitter memory?

She moved away from the door, found a light blue summer dress in her wardrobe, and changed into it. She combed her hair, put on more lipstick, and was ready. As she walked down the stairs Boris was waiting at the foot, and he looked up at her.

'I'm sorry about that,' he said. 'It never occurred to me that my father would even notice your lack of a ring.'

'And now we're going to buy one?'

'Yes.'

'Did you speak to the doctors?'

'I did. They're going to give him a detailed examination. I will phone Roberts later. Are you ready to leave?'

'Yes.'

He walked across to the front door. A silver Mercedes sports car waited outside. 'We'll travel faster in this,' he said. Polly looked at it, long, sleek, fast looking, and made a little moue of appreciation.

'This is yours as well?'

'Yes. You drive?'

'Occasionally.'

'Do you want to drive this?' She looked at him, seeking mockery, and flushed slightly.

'I shouldn't imagine you'd trust me,' she retorted dryly.

'On the contrary, I would—in this.' The last two words softly spoken.

'No, thanks.' She slid into the low bucket seat and

he closed her door. Her feelings were a complex mixture of doubt, uncertainty—and excitement. They were going out alone, possibly for several hours, and all that had passed between them could never be forgotten. His bitter, hurtful words, the scene in his study, Janet's talk that morning, the different atmosphere in the sanctuary that was his father's room—all mingled in her mind, and she knew she must try to put them out, at least temporarily. He was a dynamic, vital man, he had kissed her, touched her, and she had known a surge of physical attraction for him that had frightened her because it had never happened to her before. And now they were alone, just the two of them, in his car.

He drove swiftly along towards the gates, and Polly realised with surprise that she had nearly forgotten the outside world in the past few days. She couldn't bear the silence, even though he was clearly concentrating on his driving. 'Are we really going to Edinburgh?' she asked him, after searching desperately for something to say.

'Yes. It's only an hour's drive.' He was already speeding down the road. Perhaps at that rate, it was only an hour away. She checked that her seat belt was securely fastened. She did it discreetly—but Boris noticed anyway. 'You're quite safe with me,' he remarked, not looking at her. 'I like speed—but I like safety as well.'

'I'm sure you do.' She tried deliberately to relax. 'After all, you were a racing driver, weren't you?'

'Yes. Only for two years, then pressure of business

made me give it up. But you'd already know that, wouldn't you?'

'No. I know very little about your career, despite what you think about me.' She wished, instantly, that she hadn't said it. She could feel an imperceptible tension fill the car. Hastily she added : 'Did your father really want me to buy a dress?'

'He said so. Of course he did.'

'But I don't like——'

'He would be very disappointed if you didn't.' His voice was harsh.

'Then I will.' She sat back in her seat. Why, oh, why couldn't they have a normal conversation? 'I offered to read to him,' she went on quickly, 'because he was talking about knowing one day I would return. I was frightened he might start asking questions I couldn't answer, so I changed the subject. He seemed so pleased, I was glad I'd done so.'

'You don't mind reading to him?'

'Of course not! I'll be delighted. I can stay there longer that way.'

'Do you find the visits tiring?'

'I did at first—only because of the unusual circumstances. But now——' she hesitated—'it gets easier. I feel as if I——' again a pause as she searched for the right words, 'I'm helping in a way I don't quite understand.' There was a question to be asked, but for the life of her she didn't know how to phrase it. 'He—I know he's—dying, but——'

'But what?'

She clenched her hands tightly in her lap. 'I don't know how to say it,' she said at last.

The next moment the car was slowing, and Boris drew into a parking place at the side of the clearway, switched off the engine, and turned to her. His face was very serious.

'Shall I say it for you?' He knew. She could see what was in her eyes. 'If—he gets better, if he doesn't die—what then?'

She closed her eyes briefly. 'Yes,' she whispered. 'How can I go?'

'When you first came to my house, it was solely to ease his last weeks—or days. We both knew that. The doctor, the nurses, myself, all knew it was a matter of time.' His green eyes were very steady on her, his face strong, filled with power. 'And yet now the change is obvious. Dr Johnson is there for a very good reason today. He—Dr Roberts, that is—thinks the miracle has happened. My father is not only recovering the power of speech, but his reflexes are becoming more normal. Roberts is a cautious medical man. He's also a very good doctor—he told me this morning that nothing like this has happened before in his experience. He was, if anything, more shaken than me.'

'Then—if he continues to make the same progress?'

'He could well be out of that room in a matter of weeks.'

Polly drew a deep breath. She was hearing now, in his calm deep words, something that she had instinctively known for a day or so. 'Thank God,' she whispered. Her eyes filled with tears. 'I don't want him to die.'

'Nor do I.' He gave a slight smile. 'I love my father very much.'

'I know.' The tension had gone. For a brief time, it was as though nothing unpleasant had ever happened. She managed a smile through the tears. His face was blurred. 'But when he does get better—won't he know, then? Won't he know who I really am?'

Silence filled the car after her words. She saw his face change. 'I—don't know,' he said at last. 'I just don't know—but Roberts seems to think——'

'Yes?' She couldn't bear the waiting.

'That it's possible, because of the massive haemorrhage, that he now sees you only as Crystal—that you have *become* Crystal to him. Do you understand what I am saying?'

Polly licked her suddenly dry lips. 'Yes,' she whispered, 'I think I do.' She put her face in her hands. 'Then how can I ever leave?' She lifted her face towards him, seeing the pain in his eyes. She wanted to wipe the pain away. He had been hurt enough. Tough though he was, he had once loved his wife, and she had betrayed him, something that could break a lesser man. 'I can't leave, can I? Not as long as he lives?'

'Can you stay?' he said harshly. 'You have your life——'

'I have, but he has now become a part of it. That wasn't the intention, I know, but it is a fact. I must stay. I know you hate me—because I'm a reporter—I know that, and accept it. But I'll stay, as long as he needs me.'

Boris's hands gripped the wheel so tightly that his knuckles were white. 'I had no right to ask,' he said.

'No. That's why I've told you. I'm not doing it for you, I'm doing it for him. I hope you understand that.' Her eyes were bright. 'Please—can we go now?'

Without another word he started the engine. And now, she thought, now I'm committed. But a kind of peace filled her.

CHAPTER EIGHT

THEY were on a quiet stretch of road, traffic passed both ways, houses were few and far between. They came to a side road and Boris turned into it, and drove, more slowly now. Polly looked at him.

'This isn't the way to Edinburgh,' she said. There had been a sign not so far back, and their road was straight on.

'No, I'm doing a detour. I'm going to take you to the castle where we were married,' he answered. 'To show you—so that, if my father asks, you will know.'

'I see.' It was eminently sensible, but she wished

she had been prepared. 'Can we go in?'

'Of course. It won't take long, though.' She looked at him, saw the hawklike profile, the way he sat, relaxed, hands lightly on the wheel of the powerful car. He was a superb driver—but then she had known he would be. And as she realised that fact, she realised something else. It was as if she knew him well, knew everything about him—yet that was impossible. She scarcely knew him at all. She looked down at the handbag on her lap. I don't know him, she thought, so how can I be so certain of some things, so sure that—she paused, trying to push certain thoughts from her mind, and moved uneasily. Dear Lord, she thought, I know how he'll make love. I know it as if he had already made love to me. Her whole body went warm; she fought for inner calm. He would be a tiger—fierce, possessive; he would be all male, the aggressor—and he would be tender as well——

'What is it?' She must have made a small sound. She looked down, and her hands were clenched so tightly on her bag that it was as if she would never be able to let it go.

'N-nothing.' She took a deep breath. 'It's warm. May I open the window?'

'Certainly. Wait.' He leaned one hand across and pressed a button. The window slid down. 'Enough?'

'Yes, thank you.' She could see the castle in the near distance. Several cars were parked on the forecourt, and a large sign proclaimed that this was Durden Castle, and open to the public. It was a sprawling granite building, massive, dignified—a place for a wedding, a romantic place. Polly caught her breath, and before she could help herself said:

'Doesn't it hurt—to come back?'

'No.' He parked at the end of a row of cars. 'Not any more.' A bored-looking attendant in a white jacket strolled across to them.

'Morning, sir—oh, Mr Leander!' It was as if he had come to life. 'Wouldn't you like to drive in, sir?'

'No, thanks, Reeves. We'll park here.' Boris slid out and came round to open Polly's door. 'This is just a brief visit.'

'I'll let Sir Hugh know you're here,' the man began, looking towards his hut, which had a telephone to judge by the wires from its roof.

'It's not necessary, thanks.' Boris raised his hand in a salute and began to walk towards the gate. Polly looked back. The man was standing watching them, a puzzled look on his face.

'You know them here?' she asked.

'Sir Hugh Murray is a friend of mine. Although the castle is now the property of the National Trust, he still lives here. I didn't particularly want to see him.' Polly knew why, but she said nothing. Her previous inner calm was shattered and she felt fragile and vulnerable.

They entered a large stone hall, and the woman sitting at a desk taking visitor's money smiled, looking startled. 'Why, Mr Leander——' she began, and faltered, seeing Polly.

'Hello, Mrs Jarvis. Can we just look round for a few minutes?'

'Of course, Mr Leander——' She seemed about to add something else, smiled, instead, and turned to a woman who had just come up with two young children, and was fumbling in her handbag. 'Can I help you?'

Boris took Polly's arm. 'This way.'

'Don't we have to pay?'

'No,' he answered. He led her along a stone passage into a large and beautiful room with tapestried walls. 'This is the drawing room. In winter Hugh and his family entertain here, but in summer it's strictly for the tourists.' The furniture was old and elegant, fully in keeping with the character of the castle. A giant vase of flowers sat in the centre of a large round rosewood table, and the room was full of their fragrance. Polly looked round appreciatively.

'I'll show you the banqueting hall,' he said. 'This way.'

It was like going back into history, to enter the high-ceilinged place, bigger than a church, to see the portraits lining the walls, the long centre table, large enough to seat a hundred people at least. A giant fireplace dominated one wall, at the end, and above the mantelpiece were a shield and two crossed swords, on the red stone wall. Polly caught her breath, peopling the room with knights and their ladies, oblivious to the dozen or so visitors wandering round, talking in whispers, as if actually in church.

'Oh, yes,' she said quietly. 'I can see——' she stopped. What could she see? Boris and Crystal sitting at the head of that table, Crystal in white gown and veil, a beautiful woman with her new husband? The room full of their guests—Boris looking at his wife with love in his eyes. Was that what she could see?

'It's a lovely room, and so large,' she said, shaken.

'Yes, it is. Heaven knows how they heated it in the old days. Now you've seen it, I'll show you the chapel.'

He led her out, taking her arm as she would have gone the wrong way at the exit. A sign said: 'Private. No Entry,' and a heavy cord between two posts blocked their way. He unfastened the cord, motioned her through, and re-fastened it, to lead her through a heavily barred door and along a wide cool corridor and out into a square courtyard. Here there were no people, only two white doves watching them from the chapel roof. He walked across the courtyard and swung open the door to the chapel, and Polly walked in.

It was cool inside, and the air was sweet from the bowl of roses on the altar table. The chapel was very simple, plain wooden pews, stone floor, mullioned windows, the large cross behind the altar of dark wood. She turned to look at him, saw his face, and turned away. His eyes were shadowed, and his face seemed to have gone pale, although it could have been a trick of the light—then he moved and walked slowly towards one of the pews. Polly stood where she was, and watched him sit down. In a sense it was as if he were alone. There was something here she had no part of. Very, very quietly she went towards the door and walked out into the sunshine. She stood blinking outside, and saw a man crossing the courtyard towards her.

'My God!' he exclaimed, then stopped. Polly looked at him, puzzled. He was tall and thin, perhaps fifty, with grey hair, wearing a tweed suit. He came towards her and smiled. 'I'm sorry,' he said. 'For a moment I thought you were someone——'

'Are you Sir Hugh Murray?'

'Yes, I am. Forgive me, but I don't——' he paused politely.

'I'm with Boris Leander. He came to show me round.' She liked this man, she liked him instinctively. 'I'm sorry if we're trespassing——'

'Not at all! My man told me Boris was here, that's why I came out. I can't have him coming here and not visiting us. Are you a friend of his?'

How did she answer that one? 'I'm working for him,' she answered. 'My name's Polly Summers.'

He put out his hand. 'How d'ye do, Miss Summers. Is Boris—er——'

'In the chapel. He'll be out in a moment.'

'Of course.' As he said it, the door behind Polly opened. 'My dear fellow,' said Sir Hugh, 'how nice to see you! Don't tell me you were going to leave without saying hello?'

They shook hands, and Boris smiled. 'Would I dare? No, to be honest, Hugh, this was just a flying visit. I brought Polly—I'm sorry, I've not introduced you——'

'We introduced ourselves, old boy,' Sir Hugh waved

his apology aside. 'I must insist you come in for a coffee at least. Helen will have my skin if she knows I've let you go.' He took Polly's arm. 'This way, me dear.' She looked helplessly at Boris, knowing in a strange way what was going through his mind. He smiled.

'We can't stay long,' he said. 'But thanks. I'd like to see Helen again.' Their host led the way across the courtyard and through another door leading into the hallway of what was obviously an apartment of the castle.

A woman sitting doing a tapestry in a small, cosily furnished living room looked up as they went in, then rose to her feet, smiling.

'Boris! By all that's wonderful. We were only talking about you at breakfast. How are you, my dear?' She came forward and kissed him warmly.

'The young devil was trying to slope off without seeing us,' said her husband.

'You put it baldly—Helen, may I introduce Polly Summers? Polly—Lady Murray.' They shook hands, and Polly saw that now familiar flash of awareness in the older woman's eyes, quickly dispelled as she said in a gentle voice:

'How nice to meet you. Do sit down. You'll both have coffee?'

'Please.' Polly seated herself on the window seat, and watched the three of them. Clearly all were old friends. Sir Hugh was busying himself opening a sideboard, lifting out cups and saucers while his wife said to Boris:

'You don't come often enough to see us, you know. Tell me, how is your father at the moment?'

Boris sat down. It was as if, quite suddenly, he had come to a decision. He looked at Lady Murray who stood waiting for his answer as if poised to go out to the kitchen. 'He's much better,' he said slowly. 'I think, Helen, you'd better put that kettle on. I've got something to tell you—it will take time, but it's only fair you should know. It involves Polly.' He looked across at Polly as their two hosts looked at one another in bewilderment—mingled, perhaps, with a kind of foreknowledge of what was to come. Polly,' he said, 'do you mind if I tell them?'

She shook her head. 'No,' she said softly.

Lady Murray returned from the kitchen. 'Kettle on. Go on, Boris, what is it?'

He told the story clearly, without pause, save for the moment that Lady Murray dashed out to switch the kettle off, and they listened intently, never once interrupting until he had finished.

'My God,' said Sir Hugh. 'I knew as I crossed that yard—I knew. It was like Crystal standing there.' He turned to Polly and smiled gently. 'Boris has a lot to thank you for. We're all extremely fond of old Boris —we really thought——' he shrugged heavily, 'that it was the end—but that such a thing should happen,' he shook his head. 'Incredible!'

'He's not out of the wood yet.' Boris rubbed his forehead. 'But the change is remarkable. To hear him talking, almost normally——'

'Is indeed a miracle,' Sir Hugh said quietly. 'I really think we all need something stronger than coffee, me dears. Polly—I hope I may call you Polly?—what will it be? A brandy, sherry—what?'

'A sherry, please.' She smiled at him, feeling the warmth of these two gentle people surrounding her. Boris had not mentioned anything about her job.

'Same for me, please, Hugh—a small one, I have to drive to Edinburgh.' He paused. 'Father noticed Polly wasn't wearing a ring. We're going to buy one—she told him I was having it made smaller.'

Sir Hugh handed them all their glasses. 'Your father's health,' he toasted. They all drank. 'We'd like to come and see him, you know. Wouldn't stay long, just a quick visit to say hello.'

'That would be nice. Can I ring you when I've spoken to the doctor? You and Helen must come for dinner at the same time. Perhaps in a couple of days?'

'Delighted. Must you go to Edinburgh now? We're having lunch in a couple of hours——'

'I'd love to stay, and I'm sure Polly would, but I'd really like to get off now. The sooner we get our shopping done, the sooner we'll be back home. But I promise, Hugh, I'll phone you tonight.'

'See that you do dear,' Lady Murray said. 'We shall look forward to our visit.'

Boris put down his empty glass and stood up. Polly followed suit, and waited her cue to leave. Boris kissed . Lady Murray, shook Sir Hugh's hand, who then turned to Polly and took her hands in his. '*Au revoir,* my dear,' he said. 'Thank you for what you're doing.'

His wife came forward, seemed about to take Polly's hand, then on impulse, kissed her cheek. 'Goodbye, Polly,' she said, her eyes glowing. 'We'll see you soon.'

'Yes. Goodbye for now. Thank you for the drink.' They went out, watched by the couple on the step, and back into the castle. In silence they walked along the corridor, out through the banqueting hall, main lounge, and entrance hall, then into the sunshine.

Over to the car, he opened her door for her, and the next minute they were driving out, Boris giving an answering salute to the car park attendant as they left, then they were on the road travelling swiftly back to join the Edinburgh traffic.

At last he spoke. 'I had not intended to tell anyone, outside the house,' he said. 'But once we were there, it was difficult not to. They are both very good friends—and both had noticed the remarkable likeness. I had no choice.' He glanced steadily at her.

'I didn't mind,' she answered. 'I like them both. It seemed—right, somehow.'

'Yes, I know. If I had had to tell anybody, it would have been them. And now they will come and visit, and see for themselves how much better he is.'

'You didn't mention I was a reporter.'

'It wasn't relevant.'

'It is to you,' she answered. Boris looked at her sharply, then he pulled the car up at the side of the road.

'All right,' he said, 'and what does that mean?'

'You surely know.' She looked at him. Reaction at seeing the castle—the place where he had been married, had hit her belatedly. She had a feeling of intense hurt that she didn't recognise—yet. She was soon to realise what it was. 'The least you can do is tell people the full story——'

'The full story? Do you think they'd care what you were?'

'No. Because it's not important. It's a pity you didn't realise that as well. It doesn't affect what I'm—I'm trying to do for your father——' she stopped, aghast. What was she saying?

'I've never said it has, have I?'

'Then why did you attack me so viciously when you found out?' she lashed out. She wanted to stop, but couldn't. 'I won't forget that in a hurry——' She gasped into silence as he caught hold of her suddenly.

'Damn you!' he grated. Then the world was blotted out as he kissed her violently and roughly, fingers digging into her arms as his mouth bruised hers with a savage intensity. She struggled, but vainly, against the sudden attack, fighting for breath against a force she had never known before.

'Ah——' it was all she had time for before he kissed her again, this time forcing her head back against the seat, hands no longer on her arms but on her body, caressing her with a roughness and expertise that excited her oddly. Then suddenly she was matching his force, her hands, no longer imprisoned, going up to hold his head, to hold him to her, her nails in his hair, body arching to press against him, her whole being afire. She cried out something, she knew not what, and he drew his face back a mere inch or so, enough for her to see the deep dark excitement in his face, to see what she knew now she had been aching to see all along. At that moment she was the central pivot of his whole mind and body—her, just her. Nothing else existed for him.

'Oh, God, I want you——' it was a throaty murmur, but she heard, and was filled with the heady sense of power she had so long known in him. Then the spell was broken, shattered into a million fragments as a motorbike sped past close, too close, rocking the car slightly, and a horn tooted derisively—and Polly was suddenly, icily sane. She reached up to push him away, horrified at herself.

'You're mad!'

'If I am, so are you——' his face was white with shock, and he put his hand to her cheek, to jerk her to him, and she gasped:

'No. Leave me be!' She hit his hand away. 'Don't touch me!' Her eyes were wide. 'You kissed me—you were like an animal——' she put her hand to her bruised mouth. 'You hurt me!'

'I could hurt you more if I tried.' Excitement turned to anger, his eyes were dark with it, and she sensed the leashed power, scarcely under control, saw the muscle move in his cheek, and was afraid.

'I'm sure you could,' she shot back, hiding the fear. 'But you're not going to——'

'Not here. Not yet.' He turned away from her and jabbed in the cigar lighter button.

'Is that a threat?'

'It's a promise,' he said harshly. He reached in his glove compartment, hand as steady as a rock, and Polly watched him. Her fear turned to anger with him, and she reached out and knocked the packet of cigars from his hand.

'You won't get the chance,' she whispered. 'I know what you want—you made that very obvious.' She forced a laugh. 'You don't imagine you're the first one who's tried it on, do you? Men! You make me sick!' He bent to pick up the cigar packet, every move slow and deliberate.

'Don't do that again,' he said.

'I'll do what I want. You're not my master,' she retorted.

'Be careful. My patience is wearing thin——'

'Patience? You don't know the meaning of the word. You're like a savage——'

He caught her wrist and twisted it so that she was forced to face him. 'Am I?' he mocked. 'I promise you, you've not seen anything yet——'

'And I don't want to. Let go of my hand!' She tried to prise his fingers off. 'Let me——' He tightened his grip instead and Polly, incensed, lashed out with her free hand and caught him a stunning slap on his cheek.

'You bitch!' he grated. The next moment she was fighting him like a wildcat, pummelling, hitting—for moments only. She was caught and held in a grip of steel, pressed tightly against him, totally helpless. Then he kissed her again.

The kiss went on, and it was so different from the ones before. It was a world different. It was sweetness, and fire, and aching and longing; his lips searched hers and imprisoned hers to him and it seemed as if it would go on for ever, and she couldn't move, or struggle, but now she didn't want to.

When he was done, he moved away and looked deep into her eyes, deep into her very mind, and he said, oh, so softly: 'That is how I will make love to you—and you won't struggle to escape then, either,' and he smiled, a spark of fire in his eyes, and he added: 'And that is a promise too.' Then he released her, turned away, and started up the engine.

Polly sat there, stunned, very still, very quiet as the car roared into life. She was incapable of speech or movement. Boris started the car on its journey and drove swiftly back towards the main road.

She would never be the same again. Not now. And, looking at him as she sat in a discreet cubicle in an Edinburgh jeweller's, she thought, neither will he. She wasn't sure what had happened in the car that had changed things, but it was as if life had taken on an extra dimension; an edge, a sharpness and clarity. Boris was talking to the jeweller, a tray of wedding rings had been produced, and Polly had one on her finger and was looking at it. Boris looked at her. 'Well,' he said, 'do you like that one?' There was a glint of deep mockery in his eyes, unnoticed by the jeweller, and he reached over to take Polly's hand with his own, and she felt the leashed strength in those fingers, excitement surge through her at the tingle of his touch. It was the touch of fire. And he knew. He caressed her fingers, as though he were her lover, and the little jeweller coughed, and turned away. 'Er—there are matching engagement rings?' he said gently.

'I'd like to see them, please.'

Polly looked up as the man vanished. She had never asked if Crystal wore an engagement ring as well. 'Do we——' she began.

'Yes, we do.' He released her hand and she flushed, realising too late that there had been no need for him to hold it, and he laughed.

'If you insist,' she said coldly.

'I do.'

'They don't know you here, do they?'

'No,' he said softly. 'Why do you think I came?'

At that moment the man returned with a tray of glittering diamond rings. Boris seemed to be searching for one, picked one out and handed it to Polly. 'Try that, darling,' he said.

She knew. He had been looking for one similar to Crystal's. She saw the price on the tray and nearly fainted. Dear God, she thought, he can't buy that just to keep up a pretence—she turned to tell him, and he slipped the ring on her finger. It fitted perfectly.

'That is the one I would like you to have—but only

if you like it,' he said. It was as clear a way as anything of telling her that *that* was the one she was getting.

'It's beautiful,' she whispered.

'I'll take them both.'

'Thank you, *sir*.' The jeweller whipped away the trays and vanished behind the curtain. Her next surprise came as Boris pulled a wad of notes from his pocket and began to peel off hundred-pound notes as though they were singles. She gazed transfixed. She had never even seen a hundred-pound note in her life, hadn't even been sure they existed. She closed her eyes, and heard him laugh.

Five minutes later they were out in the street, she still dazed, the rings in two small boxes in her handbag. 'Now, for your dress,' said Boris, and ushered her along the pavement towards Princes Street.

'No,' she said.

'No?' he frowned.

'I need a cup of coffee first.'

'For shock? What did you think I would do? Pay by cheque—and have everyone know I was buying a wedding ring?'

That hadn't occurred to Polly. She shook her head. 'I suppose——' she began. Then: 'That other assistant —the one by the door as we went out—did he *know* you?'

He looked down at her and frowned. 'What made you say that?'

'He looked startled—I thought he was going to speak.'

'I didn't notice him,' he said dismissively. 'You want coffee? Very well, we'll go into this hotel. I have no intention of queueing up in a self-service café for you or anyone.'

'No, you wouldn't,' she agreed sweetly. 'Pity, you might meet some ordinary people for a change.'

He didn't answer. He just ignored the remark as if it had never been said. They went into the foyer of a large hotel, across into a lounge where people talked quietly, sitting on long comfortable settees and drinking coffee.

'Is that all you want—coffee?' he asked her, as a waiter hovered.

'Yes.'

'Two coffees, please.' The waiter vanished, and Boris turned to Polly.

'I want to be back for lunch,' he said, 'even though we'll be late. I have a lot of work to get through today.' The episode in the car might never have happened. Yet there was a difference—even in him. Nothing she could pinpoint, but it was there all the same; a subtle change, an awareness, a heightening of the tension that was invariably sparked off when they were together. It added a clarity to everything. Colours seemed sharper, brighter. Polly looked round her at the other coffee drinkers. Women's heads had turned when they had entered, and she knew why. She had seen them both in a large mirror as they had walked in, and had caught her breath in sudden shock. We look—married, she had thought. And no doubt about it, Boris Leander was a most attractive-looking man. Head and shoulders taller than Polly, and she was tall herself, and moving with a grace and power that would cause any woman's head to turn, yet it was clear he didn't give a damn whether anyone looked or not. He was probably too used to causing similar reactions wherever he went.

But to sit with him, in a public place, and to be the centre of attention, however discreet, was something Polly found stimulating. They didn't like each other, their only bond was his father, Boris had treated her violently and brutally—and yet—— She looked across the settee at him as he spoke to the waiter, and paid. What was it about him? He was the most dynamic man she had ever encountered. Dynamic, vital—virile. And, in company, impeccably mannered.

'Sugar, Polly?' he was asking her.

'No, thanks.' She gave a sweet, friendly smile to a middle-aged overdressed matron who had been frankly weighing Boris up, then turned the smile on Boris. He caught the tail end of it, and one eyebrow went up quizzically.

'It wasn't for you,' she told him pleasantly. 'I was smiling at a woman over there.'

'Do you know her?'

'No,' she said. 'But she's been staring at *you* for long enough.'

'People often do,' he said casually. 'She's probably nothing better to do.'

'How true,' she murmured.

He laughed. It was a laugh of sheer enjoyment.

'You've a fine sharp tongue on you when you want, haven't you?'

'I try to keep my wits about me, especially in your company,' she retorted, needled by his amusement. 'It's difficult at times.'

He regarded her very levelly, very coolly, until she thought she wouldn't be able to bear it a moment longer. 'Stop staring,' she said at last, aware that her cheeks had gone pink.

'I was just trying to see what makes you tick. There's a strong personality in there somewhere.'

'You should know one when you see one.' She could look calmly back at him now. 'Stare if you like.' Their eyes met, the cool green ones, hers darker, blue, and suddenly it was as if everything else faded away. Just the two of them, in a clash of wills. Then he smiled, very slowly, he smiled, and that smile held all the meaning in the world. It was Polly who looked away then, confused.

'Drink your coffee,' he said softly. 'Then we'll go.'

Silently, her mind a turmoil of mixed emotions, she did so.

CHAPTER NINE

THEY arrived back at Leander House just after two o'clock, and while Polly went to tell Janet, Boris went to telephone Dr Roberts. Over their late lunch he told her the results of the doctor's examination.

'They are both agreed that my father is improving, and not deteriorating. They don't really understand it, but think it's very probably due to your arrival here,' he said. 'They're having a physiotherapist come today, later on, to make my father exercise to regain the use of his limbs. The idea is, very cautiously at first, to see how it goes. They said——' here he gave a little smile, 'my father told them he wasn't seeing any damned physio unless you were there.'

She laughed. 'Of course I will be, if that's what he wants. That's marvellous. If he's strong enough to *argue*——'

'Yes,' he said quietly. 'Precisely. That point struck them too.'

'What time does he want me?'

'About six, Dr Roberts said.'

'Then I'll change into my new dress first. I promised I would. In fact, I'll go earlier.' She looked at her watch. 'Will you show me where the Sherlock Holmes books are? I'll begin reading today.'

'As you wish.'

She put her knife and fork down on her plate. 'I don't want any more to eat. I'm not hungry.'

'Let's go now,' he said, and stood up.

'But you've not finished——' she began.

'I'm not hungry either.' He opened the door for her and she went into the hall, and waited for him to lead the way into the library.

There he took her to a row of books on the shelf. 'Take your pick,' he said. 'They're all here.'

'All right, I'll browse for a few minutes. You go and do what you have to do. Oh, and don't forget to telephone Sir Hugh.'

'I won't.'

'The evening they come for dinner—will it be all right if I eat in the kitchen with Janet and Tom? I know I could have the meal in my room if I wanted, but I like her company——'

'What do you mean?' he cut in.

Polly stared at him. 'I—I—get on with her——'

'Not that!' He waved his hand dismissively. 'What's this about meals in your room? You'll be dining with us.'

'Oh, no, I couldn't,' she gasped. 'They're your friends——'

'And will expect to see you. Good God, woman, you've met them. What are you afraid of?'

She felt herself flush at his abrupt manner. Temper rose. 'I'm not *afraid* of anyone,' she retorted hotly. 'But I'm hardly a member of the family, am I?'

'You're a guest.'

'Yes—under protest. Your protest. You'd have booted me out if you could, when Mrs Harris did her spot of eavesdropping. They'll wonder where *she* is. Do you expect me to sit there while you tell them you sacked her—and why?' her eyes sparkled angrily. 'No, *thanks*!' She turned away from him, unable to stand still any longer, and the next moment he caught her arm.

'I'd like to spank you, you little spitfire!'

'Don't start that again.' She whirled back on him, trying to free her arm. 'Try and behave as though we're in your father's room. You're very different there.'

'And so are you,' he said grimly. 'My God, what a temper!'

'Yes!' she sparked back. 'But not as bad as yours, not by a long chalk!' The tension crackled like electricity between them. She fiery, pink-cheeked, eyes blazing; he, hard, still controlled, powerful—yet with that threat of violence simmering beneath the surface ready to erupt at any moment. No man had ever affected her thus before, had ever brought her to the wild brink of temper she experienced with him. She jerked her arm free from his grip. '*And* you're a bully!' she added recklessly, rubbing her arm. 'You use your strength——'

'You don't do so badly on that score yourself,' he said. 'You pack quite a good punch for your size——'

'Oh, go to hell!'

'If I do, I'll take you with me,' he grated. They stood facing one another, he hard-faced, she with chin tilted defiantly, both at explosion point.

Then Janet walked in. 'Oh—I'm sorry,' she said, and began to move back to the door. Boris turned.

'Yes?'

'A telephone call from London for you, sir—b-but I'll tell them you'll ring back.' Quite clearly she sensed the force in the room and was intent on escape. Polly couldn't blame her.

'I'll come now. Who is it?'

'A Mr Hulton from your New York office—he's here.'

'Yes, I know.' Boris walked out. 'Thank you, Janet.' Then he was gone. Janet stared at Polly, her eyes wider than wide.

'Did I interrupt something?' she whispered.

'And how!' Polly sank into a chair. 'Just a minor punch-up, that's all. I need a cup of tea or something.'

'I'll get you one now.'

'Thanks.' Polly watched her go, then stood, went over to the bookshelves, found *The Speckled Band*, and lifted it down. Carrying it over to an armchair, she sat down to await Janet's return. She couldn't read, not yet. Instead she looked towards the window, seeing only Boris's face as it had been in those moments before Janet came in. In a blinding flash of realisation, she knew. She knew why he could so affect her, she knew why her defences were up the moment they were alone. She knew the reason for everything. She knew she was in love with him. It was total, reckless, all-consuming. And it was so painful she could hardly bear it.

She went to her room and had a shower, then changed into the new dress, and looked at herself in the long mirror. It was the most beautiful she had ever seen. As soon as the assistant had produced it, she had known it was the one. Full-length, of softly swirling silk in muted blues and greens, it flowed, emphasising her slender figure; the low scooped neckline revealing the gentle curve of her breasts. The halter neck fastened at the back in a tiny diamond clasp. She twirled and turned to see the sideways effect, and knew she looked lovely in it.

She smiled softly, remembering Boris's face when she had tried it on and walked out of the fitting room to show him. 'Very nice,' he had said. 'Is that the one you want?'

'It is.' The glimpse had been brief, but it had been there. She had seen the shock—just for one instant of time—of naked desire in his eyes. It was enough.

She never envisaged owning a dress like that in her wildest dreams. It was totally beyond her price range, an original, nearly three hundred pounds, and she had had no intention of anything in that bracket when they had entered the store. She had made for the rail of dresses that were moderately priced, and he had touched her arm and pointed.

'Over there,' he had said. Polly looked. 'Exclusive models,' the sign said.

She laughed. 'Not there,' she protested. 'They cost a bomb——'

'My father wants you to have a dress. The cost is immaterial.'

'But I——' she began, but he took her arm, guided her over to the softly lit alcove, and said to the woman assistant waiting there:

'We would like to see some of your dresses, please.'

'Certainly, sir. This way, madam, please——' They had left him waiting, and the saleswoman, after a swift summing up glance at Polly, assessing her size, had produced, from a glass-fronted wardrobe, the dress she now wore. And that had been that. But not quite all. When the dress was wrapped Boris said:

'I think a stole to match—and sandals, and evening bag——'

'No,' protested Polly, 'really——' but nobody listened to her. She picked up the gossamer-fine stole and draped it round her shoulders now. As delicate as a spider's web, of silver, it was perfect. She flung it on the bed and went to the dressing table to make up.

Half an hour later she walked into old Mr Leander's room, crossed over to his bed, and kissed him. 'I got my dress, Poppa,' she said. 'Do you like it?'

She stood back slightly to let him see, and saw the smile that lit his face. 'Ah, yes—how beautiful you are,' he whispered.

'Thank you. It's the most lovely present you could

have bought me.' She sat down beside him. 'I've brought a book to read to you. Would you like me to read now, or later?'

'Now, but only if you wish it.'

'Of course I wish it. Tell me when you want me to stop. You know the doctors are very pleased with you—but I mustn't let you get tired.'

'They're sending someone to make me do exercises,' he said. 'I told them—only if you were here.'

'I know.' She laughed. 'I'll be here, don't worry. I'm not having anyone bullying you.'

He patted her hand. 'You look after me well, Crystal. I can't tell you how happy you've made me. I knew you'd come back. I knew—I prayed for your return——'

'And here I am,' she said softly, but her heart beat faster. There must be no questions that she couldn't answer. 'Your prayers were answered. We called at the Castle today, just a quick visit, and saw Hugh and Helen—they're going to come to dinner soon. Boris told them how much better you were.'

'Ah, yes, I haven't seen them for a while. That will be nice.' The subject had been safely changed.

Polly opened the book and began to read to him. She had told the nurse she would be there for a while, when she went in, and she had gone off for tea. When she heard the outer door open she assumed it was the nurse returning—until Boris walked in, soft-footed. Polly looked up, faltering, losing her place on the page. She had not seen him after the fight in the library—

and since her realisation that she loved him. For a moment she couldn't speak, and her heart thudded so loudly she feared they both must hear it. If this was what love was like, it was agony. She watched him cross to his father and greet him, and each second was a sweet pain to her, seeing him, his face, the expression on it, the tenderness he had never shown her, the gentleness with which he touched his father's hand. 'Hello, Father,' he said. 'I knew Crystal would be here. Doesn't she look beautiful in that dress?'

'She does indeed, my son. You must be very proud to have such a lovely wife.'

'I am.' Boris looked at Polly and smiled a tender smile. She looked at the book on her knee, helpless. To save her life, she couldn't have returned that smile. 'I only called in to say Dr Roberts phoned. The physiotherapist is on his way now.'

'Send him up when he arrives. I'll be here,' said Polly, and put her finger on the page, having found her place, then she looked up at Boris, silently willing him to go.

He nodded as if the message was only too clear. 'I'll let you get on with the book, darling,' he said—but his eyes belied his tone. Then he left them. Polly read on, becoming calmer as she slipped easily into the other world of the book, and had forgotten the time when a knock came at the door and the nurse popped her head in. The first thing Polly noticed, as she looked up, was the blush on the nurse's cheeks.

'He's here, Mr Leander,' she said, then to Polly, 'May I come in and take Mr Leander's jacket off?'

Polly stood up. 'Of course.' She watched the nurse go over to the bed, and went out of the room—and saw a tall, good-looking young man taking his coat off. He turned, saw her, then smiled. She saw the startled delight in his eyes, the smile broadened, and he spoke.

'Hello,' he said. 'I'm John Trayner. You're—er——' a brief look at the closed door to the bedroom—'Miss Summers?'

'Yes. But in there I'm Mrs Leander. You understand?'

He nodded. 'Dr Roberts told me.' His eyes were very warm, and a nice shade of blue, and he grinned as he said:

'I'm glad you're not.'

'Sorry?' but she had to grin back, because there was something irresistible about his expression.

'Glad you're not married.'

'Oh.' Her smile faded.

'I'm sorry.' He looked contrite. 'Was that impertinent of me?'

'Somewhat.' She looked at him. 'I think we'd better go in, don't you?'

'Yes.' He picked up a small black bag from the chair, and a white jacket, and followed her in, and didn't see Polly's secret smile to herself. She was glad she had her new dress on.

She seated herself again and watched John Trayner approach the patient in the bed. His face was patiently

resigned as he said: 'Now, young man, no torture.'
The nurse winked at Polly and went out.

'I promise you, sir, I shall be very gentle.' He opened
the bag to reveal neatly lined bottles and jars and
tubes, selected a bottle of oil and took it out. 'Today
I'll just massage you, see how your muscles respond.
If at any time I hurt you, let me know.'

'I will.' The old man's eyes flickered to where Polly
waited. 'My daughter-in-law is here to look after me.'

John Trayner grinned at her. 'Then I'll be extra
careful,' he said gently. He was clearly an expert at his
job, and Polly relaxed, sensing the good he would be
able to do for the man for whom she now felt a great
personal responsibility. Some minutes later he was finished. Polly helped Mr Leander on with his jacket, and
John said: 'That was excellent. Tomorrow we can start
exercises. What time is most convenient for me to
come?'

'I'll ask the nurse to come in.' Polly opened the door
and called her. She smoothed down her hair and
straightened her cap as she went in the bedroom.

'What time shall Mr Trayner come tomorrow?' Polly
asked her.

'About eleven is best.' The nurse smiled at him shyly.

'Eleven it is.' He picked up his bag. 'Nurse, see that
Mr Leander is comfortable. I think one more pillow can
be allowed during the day—Mrs Leander, may I have
a word with you outside?'

'Certainly.' She followed him out and closed the door
behind her. 'What is it?'

He looked at her. 'Will you have dinner with me tomorrow night?'

'Good heavens!' he took her breath away. 'You're a fast worker, aren't you?'

'No, but I don't beat about the bush. Will you?'

Polly looked at him. Why not? There was no harm in it. 'All right,' she said. 'We'll arrange a time tomorrow.'

'Good.' He took off his white jacket and put on his coat. 'I'll see you at eleven in the morning.'

'Yes. I'd better see you out——'

'It's all right, I'll find my way. *Au revoir*, Miss Summers.'

'Polly.'

'Polly? I like it. *Au revoir*, Polly.'

'*Au revoir.*'

She stifled a giggle and went back into the bedroom. And there she read to her 'father-in-law' until it was time to go for dinner.

She hadn't planned how to tell Boris, but her perfect opportunity came when they were seated for dinner, and Janet had served their soup, and she looked across the table towards him and said: 'The physiotherapist is very good. He's coming at eleven tomorrow.'

'Fine. I imagined they'd send a woman.'

'So did I,' she agreed. 'But he'll do your father a great deal of good. Did you phone Sir Hugh, by the way?'

He looked surprised at her apparent sudden change of subject. 'No. Why?'

'Oh, good. I don't know whether you were planning to ask them tomorrow, that's all. Only I'm going out to dinner.' Her words fell into a peculiar kind of silence that grew and grew, until——

'You're going out to dinner?' he said, face expressionless.

'Yes.' It was worth it, it was well worth accepting the young physiotherapist's invitation, just to see the expression on Boris Leander's face.

'May I ask with whom?'

'Yes. With John Trayner, the physiotherapist.'

'Do you know him?' He broke a piece of bread roll off and buttered it.

'I didn't before he came. I do now.'

'And do you make a habit of going out with men you've only just met?' he asked.

'I did with you. I went for lunch,' she pointed out, reasonably enough, she thought. His eyes met hers. They were hard, icy.

'There was a difference.' His voice was as glacial as his eyes. 'I had a proposition.'

'So you did,' she answered. She was filled with a kind of reckless bravado. He had broken that bread roll as though he would have liked it to be her neck. 'It'll be funny if *he* has a proposition for me, won't it?' and she smiled. Boris didn't. And she knew that he was icily, *furiously* angry. In a way it was worse than what had happened in the library.

'I was thinking of asking the Murrays for tomorrow,' he said, and the moment of—fear, almost—passed.

'That's all right. It's you and your father they're coming to see,' she said.

'Nevertheless they will expect you to be here as well,' he answered.

'As I would like to be, now I've been invited,' she responded. 'So why don't you make it the following night for them?'

'It looks as though I may have to.' The anger seemed to have passed. At least it was under control.

'Nobody's forcing you,' she said. 'And I wasn't aware that I was to be at your beck and call twenty-four hours a day. When I came here you told me I was to have as much time off as I wanted.' She finished her soup and put the spoon neatly on the plate.

'I am responsible for you while you are here.'

'And I'm over twenty-one, believe it or not,' she retorted. 'And quite capable of deciding for myself if I want to go out with a man.'

He seemed about to reply when Janet wheeled in the dinner trolley, with the maid, and served them. 'I'll leave the cheese and biscuits on here, Mr Leander,' she said. 'Will you ring when you need me?'

'We'll serve ourselves, thank you, Janet.'

Then they were alone again. They finished the meal in silence, and Polly rose. 'I don't want any cheese and biscuits,' she said. 'I'm going to my room, then I'll go in to see your father and read to him again. May I phone home?'

'Yes. Don't go yet, I want a word with you first.' She

stood waiting by her chair as he got to his feet and walked round the table towards her.

'What about?' She knew, of course. It would be another side-swipe at her for accepting a dinner invitation without his permission. It only made her the more determined to go.

'Not in here, in my study. It's more private.'

'Look, if you're going to start about me having a date——'

He looked at her, and the look silenced her. 'It is not about that,' he said. 'Will you go into my study?'

'No. You can say what you have to here. We only manage to fight every time we're alone. Perhaps it's best if we stick to meeting for meals—and in your father's room. I can only take so much violence——'

'There will be no fighting, I assure you. But what I have to say is very private, and extremely important.' He looked at her. 'I am asking you—please.' His face softened fractionally.

Oh, I love you, she thought. I love you and it hurts me—and I hate myself for loving you, but it doesn't make any difference. And if only you knew, how you'd laugh! If only you knew I only said yes to John Trayner to try and make you jealous. And all I did was make you angry.

'Very well,' she said, and opened the dining room door.

Boris ushered her into his study and closed the door behind them. 'I'll be brief,' he said. 'Will you sit down?'

'No, I'll stand.'

'I have spoken again to Dr Roberts this afternoon—after I saw you and my father. I asked him to tell me frankly, and off the record, what he thought of my father's chances of almost total recovery.' He smiled very slightly. 'I can be quite persuasive when I choose——'

'I'm sure you can,' she said softly.

'I did it deliberately. I made him tell me.' He paused. Polly's heart beat faster.

'And——?' she whispered.

'He thinks—he is convinced, that in another six months my father will be walking, and talking nearly as well as he did before. He and Dr Johnson had a long talk after they left, and both are agreed. They are neither of them given to making rash predictions, as you know, and I believe that what they say is true.'

'Thank God,' she whispered.

'Yes,' he said softly, 'I know. And I know what you told me—that you are prepared to stay, for which I am grateful. But I cannot ask you to do this—cannot expect you to live here, pretending to be my wife, and having to act as my wife to him when he is up and about, when he would be expecting us to share a room, to be entertaining, you to be the mistress of the house, and it all a pretence. He has been a prisoner in that room, and it has been easy. It will not be so soon. You have given up your time to come here, and whatever the friction between us, for that I am grateful. More than grateful. In a way, I owe you his life.' He paused, his face shadowed with something like pain. 'Polly,

I have a further proposition to put to you. Please listen carefully. It is the only way I can ask you to stay here any longer. Will you marry me?'

She sat down abruptly. Ashen-faced, she looked at him. He went over to the drinks cupboard and poured cognac in a glass, and handed it to her.

Polly sipped it slowly, feeling the numbness passing slightly. Then she found her voice. 'How can you marry someone you dislike so much?' she whispered.

'It will be a marriage in name only—that is what you would wish, I know,' his voice was harsh and hard. 'But you will legally be Mrs Leander, you will have all the money you need——'

She looked up sharply. 'Money? Do you think I'd say yes, for *money*?' she said. 'That's easy for you, to buy everything, isn't it? I'm not for sale. But to stay, when he's up and about—I know the problems there will be. I know.' She handed him back the glass. 'I don't want any more. I need a clear head, to think. Please let me think.' She leaned back on the chair, and Boris went over to the window, looking out.

'It's impossible,' she said, after some minutes' thought, during which he had not spoken. 'Too many people know that Crystal was killed—someone, one day, will accidentally say something——'

'No, he is well protected here. Only those will come who can guard the secret well. To him you *are* Crystal —you will remain so for as long as he lives. I have not told you all; I wanted to see what you would answer first. But now I see I must. My father is in his late seventies. It is inevitable that he will have another stroke in, say, two years, Dr Roberts says. That is all I ask—that you marry me for as long as he is alive, so that for the rest of his life he is a happy man. Then the marriage will be annulled. You will be free.'

Free, she thought. How can I ever be free of you? And how can I live under the same roof, sharing the same room—loving you, wanting you? 'You say we would share a room,' she said. 'But how—if this is to be in name only——'

'Come with me, please, I will show you.' Numbly she followed. This is all a dream, she thought. It can't be *real*.

At the front of the house, upstairs, he opened a door and she went into a large bedroom, elegantly furnished yet masculine. 'This is my room,' he said, 'and there ——' he crossed to a door in the wall, 'an adjoining bedroom. It was originally a nursery, but it is large enough to be comfortably furnished as a bedroom. It shares a bathroom with this. I will sleep in the smaller room, and this can be yours, but to all intents and purposes it will be ours.'

Polly sat down on the bed and looked around the room, seeing it, how it would be if he loved her, if they were truly married—not in name only—and it was like a pain, a sweet anguish.

There was something she had to know before she said anything else. 'Did you only decide to ask me because—I'd told you I had a date with John Trayner?' she asked.

'No,' he said harshly. 'I had already known what I

was going to do. But that, in a way, precipitated it. For when my father is better, how could you lead a private life, dating men? It would be impossible.'

'Yes, I see that.' She stroked the blue candlewick coverlet. 'It would be difficult—and embarrassing.' Her eyes filled with tears. She saw his father's face, the trust and affection that lit it every time she walked into his room. She had no choice, she knew that. There had been no choice all along.

'I love your father,' she said slowly. 'I have grown to love him as though he were my own father.' She looked up at him, her eyes clear and bright with unshed tears. 'And for that reason, I'll say yes.'

CHAPTER TEN

Boris and Polly were married a week later by special licence in the same chapel in which he had married Crystal.

Afterwards they ate a meal with Sir Hugh and Lady Murray, their only guests, and witnesses, and drove home to Leander House. There Polly went straight up to her new bedroom, to where her clothes had been transferred, changed out of her pale blue wedding suit, and lay down on the bed to think over all that had happened, and to try and calm herself before going in to see her new father-in-law. Because for him it had just been another day. They had told him they were driving to visit the Murrays for lunch, and she would see him when they returned.

She looked at her watch. She would go in half an hour. Time to think over the past few crowded days in her mind, and try and sort order from the chaos. It was Monday, her wedding day, the day that should have been the biggest and most important in her life, and all she felt was a kind of numbness at it all. It had been the previous Monday that they had travelled to Edinburgh for the rings, and she had bought the dress and worn it, had met John Trayner, and had her strange marriage proposal. A sufficiently traumatic day on its own—but worse was to come.

On Tuesday Janet had come up to her room, white-faced, at eight, and handed her a daily paper. 'Look at that,' she said, and pointed to a headline at the right centre of the front page. 'Wife Number Two for Leander?' it said, and underneath: 'Can the mysterious Boris Leander be considering marriage for the second time? Accompanied by a beautiful blonde, he bought a wedding ring in an Edinburgh jeweller's yesterday. An assistant who recognised the man of mystery said: "They looked radiantly happy——"' Polly flung the paper down and looked at Janet. She felt sick. 'Does he know?' she whispered.

'No, but he will. Oh, Polly, you know what he thinks about papers——'

'Not only that, he'll think it's me,' she said, agonised. 'We only went because old Mr Leander had noticed I wasn't wearing a ring——' she stopped. Janet didn't know about Boris's proposal the previous evening. He had said he would tell Janet and Tom that morning. And now, now that she had braced herself for a marriage, it would probably be off.

'I'd better speak to him,' she said. 'Where is he?'

'In his study.'

She had gone in, with the paper, prepared for she knew not what—certainly the worst. It didn't happen. He had read the piece, grim-faced, then said: 'You thought you saw an assistant staring at me?'

'Yes. I told you——'

'It was probably him. If I went in, I'd probably kill him, so I won't.'

'I thought you'd think it was me,' she said, dizzy with relief.

'I might have, a few days ago. Best forget it. Little do they know how right they are.' He had smiled, but the smile hadn't reached his eyes. 'When you go in to my father this morning, and when Trayner has finished send him down will you? I want to see him.'

Alarm flared. 'You're not going to——'

'I'm not going to give him a rocket, no. I simply want to ask him if my father needs any equipment for exercising—and to tell him that your dinner date is cancelled.'

She opened her mouth to speak, and changed her mind. 'And Hugh and Helen are coming tonight, by the way. I would like them to be guests at our wedding. Are you agreeable?'

'Yes. When can I tell Zoe? I phoned her last night, but said nothing.'

'Can I ask you not to tell them until afterwards?'

Polly had suspected as much, but she nodded. 'I— suppose so.'

'Thank you.' His face softened slightly. 'I promise— in return, they can come and stay for a few days very soon.'

'But he's on a newspaper——' she began, aghast.

'Yes, I'm well aware of that. But they are family to you, aren't they? It is the least I can do.'

'You can trust him,' she said slowly. 'I'll make him promise—not a word.'

'I know you will. Polly, will you excuse me, I have a lot to do before breakfast, including, later on, arranging a wedding.'

He was different. She thought over that as she lay on the bed now, thought how he had changed in the days that followed. Hard, impersonal; there had been no more scenes, no fights—nothing. It might have been a business deal he was arranging. And in a way that was precisely what it was. Twenty minutes had passed. She got off the bed and walked towards the wardrobe to find a summer dress, and Boris walked into the room. She stood there in her white slip and turned slowly, embarrassed.

'I'm sorry, I forgot to knock,' he said. He handed her a small gift-wrapped box.

'What is it?'

'A small wedding present for you.'

'How nice. Who from?'

'Me.' She found herself, much to her horror, going pink.

'But I didn't w-want——' she began, stammering.

'I know. This is purely a business arrangement. But it will go nicely with your long dress. Incidentally, I've opened an account for you at that shop in Edinburgh. Tomorrow—or when you choose—you must go and get anything you need in the way of clothes. Janet will go with you if you like.'

'I don't intend to spend your money,' she said.

He frowned. 'The last thing I would suggest about you is that you are a gold-digger,' he said. 'You've made your standpoint on money very clear. But as my wife, you will need a more extensive wardrobe than the one you possess. I certainly have no intention of expecting you to pay for extras like that yourself. You will also have a weekly allowance—after all, you won't have a job as such any more.'

Polly hadn't even given that fact a thought in the entire week. It was sensible. In a way she was employed by him. She nodded. 'I see. I'd like to change now, if you don't mind.'

'Of course. I'll see you at dinner.' He went out. My husband, she thought, and he's more of a stranger now than he was before. She opened the box to reveal an exquisite pendant set in white gold. The amethyst was in the shape of a teardrop, and also in the box was a pair of matching earrings. She put it down on her dressing table and closed it. It was beautiful, but it hadn't been given with love. It was an impersonal token, a symbol of a business arrangement.

She opened her wardrobe and took out a simple cotton frock. A knock came at the door, and Janet came in as Polly answered.

'I've brought you a little present,' she said, 'from Tom and me.' She handed Polly a small package.

'Thank you, Janet, how kind you are.' Polly undid the paper and opened a long white box to reveal a pretty pearl necklace.

'They're only cultured, nothing fancy, but—well, we wanted you to have something——' She stopped, shocked, as Polly burst into tears. 'What is it? Oh, Polly, what——'

'It's nothing,' said Polly, voice muffled through her sobs, 'it's such a lovely thought—thank you, Janet. You don't know what they mean to me——'

'Here, sit down on the bed. Don't take on so—why, it's your wedding day! Cook's done something special for dinner—they're all excited in the kitchen—you'd think it was their wedding!' Janet sat beside Polly and took her hand. 'Listen love, I know, I can guess, that is, why you're crying——'

'No, you can't,' Polly whispered fiercely. 'No one can.'

'Can't I? I don't miss much. I know old Mr Leander's getting better, I know you're staying, and I know why Mr Leander asked you to marry him—and I know something else. You love him, don't you?'

'Is it so obvious?' Polly whispered.

'Only to me.' She smiled slightly. 'Don't worry, your secret's safe. I won't tell—not even Tom. Now dry your tears. You've got work to do.'

'Work?'

'You're the mistress of the house now, you know. You'll have to give me orders every day.'

'Oh, Janet,' Polly laughed weakly. 'I wouldn't know where to begin.'

'You'll learn. I'll have to start calling you madam for a start——'

'Don't you dare!' But she began to feel more cheerful. She would survive. She had work to do, Janet said. She had more than one job, come to that. And the most important was being a good and loving daughter-in-law. That was the only reason Boris had married her, and she was not going to let him down. She sat up straighter. 'You've stopped me feeling sorry for myself. Thanks, Janet, I needed someone with a bit of common sense to shake me. Right, I'm the mistress of the house. Perhaps we'd better have a talk about that later. Do you like being housekeeper, or would you prefer Boris to get one?'

'I like it,' Janet answered frankly.

'Then that's decided. You stay as it. Did he give you a rise?'

'Well, no—but——'

'I'll see him.' She looked at Janet, eyes shining. 'I think he's due for a few surprises, don't you?'

Janet started to smile. 'And tomorrow I'd like Tom to take me to Edinburgh. I'm going to buy some clothes. I'd like you too come to. Can you manage to?'

Janet stood up and bobbed a curtsey. 'As madam wishes, of course.'

'I do. I insist, in fact.' They both began to laugh.

When Polly went several minutes later to see old Mr Leander, she felt much better than she had all week.

That evening after dinner she said to Boris: 'I'm going to Edinburgh tomorrow with Janet and Tom. I'd like her to stay on as housekeeper, officially.'

He looked faintly surprised, but nodded. 'I thought she already was,' he said.

'Perhaps. But it's not been made official, has it? Obviously you were paying Mrs Harris more——'

'Obviously,' he agreed drily.

'Then Janet must have a rise to bring her up to the same.'

'Very well.' He seemed faintly amused. 'Anything else?'

'Yes, quite a few things, actually. As your wife, I'm mistress of the house. I'd like new curtains in the drawing room. Those are quite old——'

'Then get them. Is that all?'

'No. As soon as I have time I'm going to go right through the house with Janet and see what needs renewing. Mrs Harris did her job well, I'm sure, but I think I can find areas where she was lacking.'

Boris looked at her across the table and put down his coffee cup. 'You're serious, aren't you?'

'Perfectly.' She stared steadily back at him.

A corner of his mouth twitched. 'Go ahead, do whatever you choose.'

'You mean that?'

'Yes.'

She stood up. 'Right, I'm going to see your father now, then I shall have an early night. I'm tired, and I'm going to be up at eight in the morning. Thank you for the pendant and earrings, it's a beautiful gift. I also had one from Janet and Tom, a pearl necklace. I was very touched by that.' She turned and walked steadily out of the room.

She lay awake in bed later, recalling her words—and the look she had seen on Boris's face as she said them. Whatever she had intended—and she wasn't sure herself what it was—the words had gone home. She felt wide awake. Her wedding night, and she was sleeping alone. Now there was no Mrs Harris to catch her heating milk in the kitchen. She could do what she liked, when she liked. She belted her new housecoat, put on her fluffy mules, and went downstairs. On her way to the kitchen she paused. Why milk? Surely on her wedding night, a bride was allowed to have a drink? She went into the dining room, switched on the lights, walked over to the cocktail cabinet and opened it.

She took out a bottle of gin and a silver goblet,

poured out a measure, and drank it. 'Here's to the happy couple,' she said quietly, and refilled the goblet. By the time she had knocked that back she felt gloriously, crazily tiddly. 'Whoops!' she giggled, as the goblet fell to the carpet. She bent to pick it up, and the room swirled round, and Boris said:

'What are you doing?' He walked slowly across towards her.

'Drinking to me,' she hiccuped gently. 'Want to join me?'

'No, thanks. I'm working.'

'Of course you are.' She smiled happily at him. 'You're always working aren't you? It must be nice to be so busy. I'm going to be very busy from now on. I have a house to run, you know.' She sat down suddenly, and he caught the gin bottle as it started to fall.

'Hadn't you better go back to bed?' he asked, quite gently for him.

'When I've had another——' She squinted for the bottle, but it wasn't there. 'Where's the g-g-gin?'

'I've put it away.'

'Then get it out again.'

'No.' She stood up.

'If you won't, I will,' she said, and reached into the cabinet for it. He caught her wrist and she knocked it violently away, glaring up at him.

'Don't touch me!' she breathed. 'Don't ever——' she turned away, but he picked her up in his arms and carried her out of the room. She kicked her legs. 'Put me down!'

'No.' He carried her silently up the stairs, and Polly lay still, strength gone, as everything swirled round. Boris pushed open the bedroom door with his foot and went in, laying her on the bed. Polly put her hands round his neck and clung on.

'Lie down,' he said, and put his hands up to ease her arms away. 'I'll get you something to sober you up or you'll have one hell of a hangover in the morning——'

'What will you get me?' she asked, and began to giggle helplessly.

'You'll see. Lie down.' She lay down obediently and watched him leave the room. Then, very carefully, she sat up and took off her dressing gown. It was very warm—too warm. Without thinking too much about what she was doing she lifted up her beautiful new pink nightgown and eased it up over her head. Then she lay down again. In a minute she would get into the bed. Before Boris came back—if he came back at all. She frowned. Had he said he was going for something? It was rather too much effort to think, so she closed her eyes, because the moon slanting into the darkened room was too bright.

She heard his footsteps outside and tried to sit up, but the room whirled round too violently. She put her hand to her forehead, and closed her eyes as he came in.

'Here——' he began, and stopped. She heard the door close, thought he'd gone, and opened her eyes to see him standing there. 'What on earth are you doing?' he demanded thickly.

She looked down at herself. 'I was warm,' she said. 'Oh, dear, I've got nothing on—where's my nightie?' She reached out for it, and he sat down on the bed, helping her up, holding her nightgown.

'Put your arms——' he began, and she leaned forward and kissed him.

'That's a kiss from the bride,' she whispered. His hands slid round to her back. She felt them, very warm, sliding round her, and she put her arms round his neck. 'I'm going to fall,' she said. 'Oh, dear——'

His mouth silenced her. Then his hands were moving, moving, so slowly, and she was lying down. His weight was on her, and he was very heavy, but he was oh, so gentle, and he said: 'You're not going to fall——' then he kissed her again, his mouth searching hers, warm, warm, tender, deeply searching, and the fire that was in her blazed into white heat, and suddenly there was no time, only a great urgency and a need and a longing. She gasped, knowing now what must happen, senses reeling with the touch from his hands, a touch that coursed through her veins and sent her pulse rocketing so that she thought she must surely die from this ecstasy.

Boris moved his body slightly, eased it away, and she heard the silken whisper of his shirt as it fell to the floor, heard a belt being unbuckled, and her body said —hurry, hurry, and her mouth said: 'No——' but softly, so softly that it would not be heard.

Then only warmth, in the darkness, and his body, hard against hers, and then it was too late for any words at all, and none were needed. Exquisite pain, and sweetness, and fire—all mingled and became one with the night, and at last, sated, they slept.

When she awoke in the dark, it was to see the blurred shadowy head on the pillow beside her. The covers were over them, and it was cooler, and Polly moved gently closer, to feel his nearness and seek his warmth, and her body tingled at the memory of his lovemaking. It was all she had ever imagined and more, much more, and she felt a great surge of love for him, as she slid her arm round him, and knew he had wakened too. He turned to face her, and took hold of her, now gently, with no urgency, only tenderness, and their lips met in a sweet kiss that went on and on until the fire was rekindled, but now at last, now there was no haste, only a delicious warmth and a gentle, mutual need.

When she awoke in the morning he had gone. Polly sat up in bed and looked around the room, seeing it with new eyes, a new awareness. She yawned and stretched, her body vibrantly alive, her whole being suffused with great happiness. This was bliss. She sang softly to herself as she showered and dressed, then went downstairs to the dining room where breakfast was laid out, as ever, in heated covered dishes. She wondered where Boris was, how long he had been up. It was barely eight. She wanted to throw her arms round him when she saw him. Perhaps she would, if they were alone....

She ate well, and Janet brought in her hot coffee, and asked with a smile what time she wanted to leave on the shopping trip.

'After I've seen my father-in-law.' It was nice to be

able to say that. 'Where's my husband?' That was even nicer to say.

'He went out early,' answered Janet. 'He has some business to attend to, he said, but he'll be in this afternoon.'

'Oh.' She must learn that there were areas of his life that were nothing to do with her, especially in business. 'Well, we'll go about ten. If he's not in for lunch, we might as well eat in Edinburgh ourselves—I'll treat you.'

'That would be very nice.'

'Tell Tom not to wear his uniform.'

'Fine. Well, I'll let you have your coffee in peace. Just ring when you're ready.'

She had a long pleasant visit to the invalid, and escaped, thankfully, when John arrived. He was well established with old Mr Leander now, and Polly's presence was no longer essential. His manner with her now was extremely formal, after hearing of her marriage—which in part was due to him, although she had no intention of telling him.

She promised to bring some more Edinburgh rock back, then went to find Janet. The house seemed empty without Boris, but she intended to be back when he returned. They set off in the Daimler, and the next hours passed swiftly in a welter of shopping along Princes Street. New curtains ordered, some clothes for Polly—not too many, she had no intention of over-spending, and finally, lunch in the restaurant of the store.

When they had eaten Polly looked at them both. She had a secret, and she wanted to be alone. She intended buying a wedding present for Boris, and she wasn't going to tell anybody. 'Look,' she said, 'I'd like a little wander round Edinburgh by myself—I'm sure you two would like a couple of hours off. Can we meet, say back here, about three, have coffee, and go home?'

Tom looked at his wife and nodded. 'That's very nice of you Mrs Leander——' he had always been more formal with Polly than his wife, 'we'd like that, wouldn't we, love? Have a look round the Castle, we can.'

'You won't get lost, will you?' asked Janet.

'No.' Polly smiled. 'And if I do, I'm big enough to ask a policeman.'

She left them in the restaurant after signing the bill, and set off with no clear idea where she was going, except that she wanted to find a small jeweller's shop and there buy something for Boris.

It was a pleasant day; tourists crowded the busy streets, and Edinburgh was truly beautiful in the sunlight. She wanted to skip along, but that hardly befitted a respectable married lady, so she walked instead, but with a spring in her step. More than one male head turned to see her pass, and two dustmen waiting at the lights in their lorry gave loud wolf whistles, which she ignored, hiding a smile.

She was in the older part of the city, with tall grey houses looming either side of the streets, and trees in small parks adding a touch of colour. She breathed deeply of the fresh summer air, and reached a crossroads. There were shops either direction. She had a choice. 'Right,' she said, and turned right. It was a decision that was to affect her life.

She had found exactly the gift for Boris. It had been in a small jeweller's shop in a side street off the main road that she had seen the gold tie-pin hidden in a corner of a case in the window, and gone in to ask the price. She could afford it—just, with her own money that she had brought with her. She paid, it was neatly wrapped, and she went out into the warm sunlight again, trying to decide which would be the quickest route back to Princes Street. Then she saw Boris. He was standing in the open doorway of one of the tall grey houses opposite talking to a woman. In the act of opening her mouth to call him, Polly froze as she saw the woman put her arms round him and kiss him. Then he closed the door, and she saw no more. It was as if her bones turned to water. She couldn't have moved then if she had tried. It must have been her imagination—it *must*. But it wasn't, and she knew it wasn't. That had been Boris talking intimately with a woman—and then going back in after kissing her, and closing the door. On leaden feet, with no clear idea of where she wanted to go, she walked on a few steps and looked across the road. The house had been the end one of a terrace, and in the street beside it, as if she needed confirmation, Boris's car was parked.

She found her way somehow back to the restaurant

on Princes Street, numbed and dazed with shock, and saw Janet waiting. 'Tom's gone for the car,' she said. 'He'll drive back in about five min——' Polly? Are you all right?'

'I've got a splitting headache,' Polly answered, with truth.

'Ah, what a shame. Anything I can get you?'

'No, I'll be all right when we get home.' She sat in the back seat with closed eyes for most of the journey, then decided that she must pull herself together. Boris must have a mistress in Edinburgh. Hardly unnatural; she had discovered for herself that he was a very virile man. It was highly unlikely that he had been the recluse the papers made out over the past five years. And after leaving my bed, she thought, he went straight to her. Which means that I—no! She gripped her hands tightly together. I must not think of anything. I must put him out of my mind, or I'll drive myself mad. Soon was the test—when they met again. And it would be soon, for they were nearing the approach road to Leander House.

Janet opened the partition. 'I'll bring you up a cup of tea and a couple of aspirin if you want to lie down when we go in,' she said.

'No, thanks. I'll be all right, really. I will have a cup of tea, though,' Polly answered. At least he wouldn't be back yet, so she would have time to compose herself. She would sit in the library and read. With any luck, she might not see him until dinner. She gazed bitterly at the house as the car approached it. How happy she had been when they left it that morning. Too happy, as it now turned out. And too stupid to see that she had merely provided a diversion for him.

'I'll be in the library, Janet,' she said, as the car drew to a halt. 'I'm looking out a couple more books for my father-in-law, then I'll probably go up and read to him before dinner.'

She left the car and ran up the steps, fumbling for the key which Boris had given her only the previous day.

Safely in the coolness of the library she sat down, after picking several books at random, and began to read.

She was sitting with old Mr Leander, talking, when Boris walked in, kissed his father, then leaned over Polly and kissed her. 'Hello, darling,' he said. 'Did you have a good day at the shops?'

She stiffened in revulsion. She couldn't help it, and he looked at her, eyes narrowing as he moved away.

'Fine, thanks. We had lunch in Princes Street.' It was all she could do to speak normally to him. 'I've bought some new curtains for the drawing room, Poppa. I didn't tell you, did I? You'll soon be coming down, so you'll see them for yourself.' She patted his hand. 'You'll like them.'

'I'm sure I will. And where've you been all day, Boris?'

'I was in Edinburgh too, as a matter of fact, on business, but I left early.'

Polly looked at her watch. 'Poppa, is that the time? I must go and have a shower and change for dinner. I'll see you afterwards. I'll leave you both to talk.' She kissed him, and fled.

She didn't have long to wait. She was changing when Boris walked into the bedroom without knocking, and closed the door behind him. 'Polly?' he said. 'What's wrong? What on earth is——'

She whirled round on him. 'You should know. You should *know*!'

'But I don't.' His face had gone hard and grim. 'You flinched as though I were a leper just there, in his room.'

'You are to me. Oh, God, I despise you! I despise myself for letting you make love to me—you're contemptible and——'

He came over and caught her roughly, shaking her. 'Stop it,' he grated. 'You don't know what you're saying! How can you——'

'I *saw* you,' she hissed. 'I went to buy a present for you—a wedding present, to give you with love—and I *saw* you——' a sob was wrenched from her—'kissing a woman, and then—then——' she nearly choked on the last few words, 'g-going back into the house——'

He suddenly released her, and she nearly fell. 'Oh, God,' he said, and his face was white. 'Polly——'

'Don't. Please don't tell me any lies,' she breathed. 'I couldn't bear it. I can't bear it now—but I'll have to. I don't want to hear any more from you. Please—leave me now.'

CHAPTER ELEVEN

'No,' he said. 'I'm not leaving this room until you've heard what I have to say.'

'Then I will.' She pulled her dress on and picked up her bag. He caught her before she reached the door and turned her to face him. Leaning past her, he bolted the door.

'No, you're not leaving either, not yet.' She stood limp and unresisting in his arms, making no attempt to struggle, looking blankly at his shirt front. Boris cupped her chin in his hand and tilted her face up so that she had to look at him.

'Listen to me,' he said. 'Just listen.'

'No, I'm not going to. I saw what I saw. I married you—a business arrangement, a marriage in name only —and I behaved very stupidly last night. It won't happen again. She's welcome to you.'

'Is she? Is she *really*? Was I mistaken then, last night? Did I imagine that what happened meant something to you?' His face was anguished. She had never seen him looking like that before. She had seen anger —and a brief pain; she had seen the hardness in him— and she had seen the gentleness when he was with his father. But she had never seen a look of despair like she was seeing now. It made her pause, as she was about to give a hasty reply, and wait.

'I—married you, Polly, for the reasons I told you. And I thought that would be it. But before—when you told me in my study that you were going out with the physiotherapist, something very odd happened—I was suddenly intensely jealous. That is the only way I can describe it. You meant—I thought you meant—nothing to me, but in that instant I knew it wasn't so.' His hands became gentler on her arms, his face showed a kind of dawning wonder. 'I realised I loved you. That's a lot for me to admit—I had decided I would never love another woman after Crystal. I was finished with love. I had loved her deeply when we were married, at first, until I discovered that she was incapable of love or fidelity.' His voice dropped, his face was nearly grey with pain. 'I am telling you this now, because I have to. Because I have to make you see. My wife was running away with another man when she was killed. She had already killed my love for her——'

'Don't,' she whispered. 'Don't torture yourself.'

'I must tell you. Then you will understand about this afternoon——'

'I don't think that matters any more,' she said shakily. 'Perhaps I was mistaken——'

'You weren't—in what you saw. But what you saw was a distortion. Sit down.' He led her gently to the bed and sat beside her. 'I wasn't strong enough to remain totally celibate—God knows, I'm no saint. That woman you saw was my mistress, but I had no intention of seeing her after we were married, even though ours is—was—going to be purely an arrangement for my father's sake. Do you believe me?'

'Yes,' she whispered.

'There was no love on either side. Let's be honest, I had the money to give her all the pretty things she wanted, and with her I sought solace and companionship. And that is all. She had been away for a few weeks, and read that item in the paper when she returned yesterday, and phoned me. I am not cruel enough to discard people without a word; I owed it to her to tell her in person. And that is why I went, after I had had a business meeting, to see her. I didn't kiss her, or touch her, that I swear. But we talked for an hour or so—I told her everything, about my father, about you, and how you had come into my life—and she took it very well, then told me why. She had found a man she was going to marry, while she had been away. We were in the hall when she told me this. I was about to leave—this is when you must have seen us, and she put her arms round me and kissed me, and said something like—"that's for old times' sake" and started to cry. I closed the door, because quite frankly I find it embarrassing to stand in full view of passers-by with a weeping woman in my arms. And that was the only reason. We weren't going in to make love. That's what you thought, isn't it?'

'Yes. Do you—blame me?'

Boris put his arms round her. 'No. But if you'd waited, you'd have seen me leave two minutes later. I was home before you. I heard you come in and go straight to the library. The only reason I didn't go into you then was because I was waiting for an important call from America. When I'd finished it, you'd gone.'

'I went up to my room to wash before going to see your father.'

'I know. I wanted to see you, but I knew I would later. Perhaps we should have sorted it out then—but I didn't know, how could I? I was going to tell you anyway, but not like this.' He held her close to him. 'I intended telling you everything, because last night, and this morning, I realised that I love you very much. You mean more to me than anything. And tonight I planned a dinner, and champagne for us both, and an early night, and plans to be made for the future——'

'Our future?'

'Yes. I want you with me wherever I go. We'll work something out. For the next two years or so it may mean spending as much time here as possible, with my father—Polly, there's something I haven't asked you. Forgive me, I've gone talking on about myself—I've never considered your feelings.'

'They're quite simple really,' she said. 'I discovered I loved you quite some time ago. But then we were always fighting——' she paused.

He grinned. 'And how! Perhaps we always will. I clearly arouse an aggressive streak in you, and you in me. But now——' he paused.

'It's the making up after that counts.'

'Yes. I think what perhaps made me realise most what you meant to me was something you said after I had given you the pendant set. You told me that Tom and Janet had given you a present of a necklace—and it was the way you said it. That hurt.'

'I know,' she said softly. 'I know——'

'Because although you were not to know it. Polly, that present of mine was given with love.' He closed his eyes briefly. 'And I was unable to express it .That will never happen again.'

'I know that too.' She turned to him, and their lips met in a long lingering kiss of sweet warmth and fire. 'Hadn't we better get ready for dinner?' she murmured, after a few minutes.

'Dinner can wait. I can't,' he said.

'But——' That was all she got the chance to say.

Dinner was very late that evening.

Harlequin
Collection

EDITIONS OF 1979

YESTERDAY'S LOVE FOR ALL YOUR TOMORROWS

You relive your love in memories. Letters tied in blue ribbon...roses pressed between the pages of a book... keepsakes of a romance that will never be forgotten.

A great love story has a different kind of timelessness. It can be cherished in memory, but it can also come alive over and over again. Harlequin proved that three years ago, when we introduced the first 100 Collections—outstanding novels, chosen from two decades of beautiful love stories. Stories that are still treasured by the women who read them.

Now we are bringing you the Harlequin's Collection editions of 1979. Best-selling romantic novels that were written from the heart, giving them a brilliance that the passage of time cannot dim. Like a lovingly crafted family heirloom or a gift from someone you love, these stories will have a special personal significance. Because when you read them today, you'll relive love. A love that will last, for all your tomorrows.

$1.25 each

Choose from this list of
classic Collection editions

Relive a great romance...
Harlequin's Collection 1979
Complete and mail this coupon today!

Harlequin Reader Service

In U.S.A.
MPO Box 707
Niagara Falls, N.Y. 14302

In Canada
649 Ontario St.
Stratford, Ontario, N5A 6W2

Please send me the following Harlequin's Collection novels. I am enclosing my check or money order for $1.25 for each novel ordered, plus 25¢ to cover postage and handling.

☐ 152	☐ 161	☐ 169
☐ 153	☐ 162	☐ 170
☐ 154	☐ 163	☐ 171
☐ 155	☐ 164	☐ 172
☐ 156	☐ 165	☐ 173
☐ 158	☐ 166	☐ 174
☐ 159	☐ 167	☐ 175
☐ 160	☐ 168	☐ 176

Number of novels checked @ $1.25 each = $ _____

N.Y. and N.J. residents add appropriate sales tax $ _____

Postage and handling $ _____.25

TOTAL $ _____

NAME _____
(Please Print)

ADDRESS _____

CITY _____

STATE/PROV. _____

ZIP/POSTAL CODE _____

Offer expires December 31, 1979

3 GREAT NOVELS

Harlequin brings you a book to cherish ...

three stories of love and romance by one of your favorite Harlequin authors ...

And there's still *more* love in

Harlequin Presents...

Yes!

Six more spellbinding
romantic stories every month
by your favorite authors.
Elegant and sophisticated tales of
love and love's conflicts.

Let your imagination be swept away to
exotic places in search of adventure,
intrigue and romance. Get to
know the warm, true-to-life
characters. Share the special
kind of miracle that
love can be.

Don't miss out. Buy now and discover
the world of HARLEQUIN PRESENTS...